The Boy at the Boundary

Anindya Sircar

BLUEROSE PUBLISHERS
India | U.K.

For permissions requests or inquiries regarding this publication, please contact:

BLUEROSE PUBLISHERS
www.BlueRoseONE.com
info@bluerosepublishers.com
+91 8882 898 898
+4407342408967

ISBN: 978-93-7018-887-7

First Edition: March 2025

The Boy at the Boundary

BlueRose ONE .com
Stories Matter
NewDelhi • London

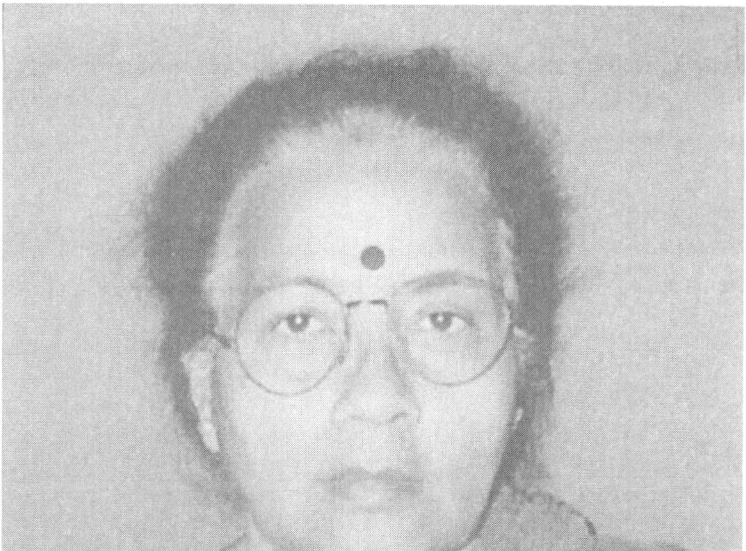

To my Maa, Mrs. Bela Sircar,

You were the angel God sent—to love, to nurture, to shape my world. In your eyes, I found the courage to dream; in your embrace, the strength to persevere.

Before I knew what a teacher was, you taught me. Before I understood the power of stories, you showed me. Your love has been my greatest lesson, your wisdom is my guiding light.

Though you have returned to your Creator, your presence remains in every step I take. I am, and always will be, your child—trying to carry forward the love, grace, and strength you instilled in me.

This book is for you—my first and forever teacher, my guardian angel, my Maa.

With eternal love and gratitude,

Your child

Contents

Acknowledgements

MY DEEPEST GRATITUDE is to you dear reader for choosing this book and taking the time to read these often-overlooked acknowledgements. Your time is truly appreciated.

I am indebted to countless individuals who have shaped my cricketing journey. This book exists because of who I am today, and for that, I owe thanks to many remarkable people.

To my Maa, Mrs Bela Sircar, my first and finest pillar of support in every way—emotionally, psychologically and physically. Her boundless love and nurturing have been the bedrock of my existence, and words cannot express her significance. Even a tome dedicated solely to her would be insufficient. Maa, wherever you are, I hope you are happy seeing your son bring this dream to life through words.

To my Baba, Dr Arjya Sircar, one of the most erudite men I have ever known. You masterfully balanced your demanding academic career while providing us a comfortable life, never compromising on precious family time. Only with maturity did I truly appreciate the magnitude of this feat. From the time I was just five or six years old, you dedicated time to play cricket with me, seamlessly transitioning into being my coach and mentor. Through you, my enduring love affair with cricket began and flourished. You imparted not merely the technical aspects but also taught me to cherish the game's very essence and entirety—its spirit, its wisdom, and its transformative power.

While this book wasn't your brainchild, my ability to articulate in English—to a standard that impressed publishers—stems from your genetic legacy. Your home tutoring, coupled with my experience of your formal university lectures, and observing you guide postgraduate and PhD students, profoundly influenced me. This was like Eklavya learning from Dronacharya, sans the *guru dakshina* of the thumb of his right hand. You remain my ultimate role model.

The earliest companions on this journey were my cricket brothers who were instrumental in charting my course. Dr Alok Singh, whose camaraderie and partnership proved not just crucial but foundational. Alongside him was Mr Sumit Upadhaya, our steadfast companion through those formative years. Without their unwavering faith in me and our shared passion, my cricketing odyssey might never have taken flight. My heartfelt thanks to you, *Bhai log.*

To my sisters, Joita Dhar and Jagori Dhar; your enthusiastic interest in my cricketing adventures brought warmth to my journey. Though not involved directly, your animated discussions about cricketers like Ajay Jadeja and Ajay Ratra added joy and levity to my path.

To my sister, Devtara Sinha, you have brought fresh perspectives to my world. Though I grew up as an only child until you entered our lives, your presence has immeasurably enriched my understanding of life's relationships.

A special tribute is due to 'Jitender *Bhaiyya*' (Jitender Singh). His mentorship and steadfast encouragement elevated my game beyond what I believed possible. His faith in me surpassed my own, instilling a confidence that helped me stand tall amongst the finest. Beyond cricket, I learned leadership, motivation, and team management—skills that remain relevant across all spheres of my life. His influence leaves an indelible mark for which I remain eternally grateful.

To that special girl who once graced my life; thank you for the beautiful memories we shared. That chapter, shaped by your presence, transformed me profoundly and remains treasured.

This book owes its existence to my dear friend, Mr Jayant Singh, who first planted the seed of authorship in my mind. Your persistent encouragement and belief ultimately bore fruit in these pages. Jayant, your friendship has been invaluable.

Thanks are due to Jayant's younger brother Vijayant, for his guidance.

I am grateful to Roopa Sharma (Roopa di) for being a guide on the journey of publishing my first book..

To my friend, Ms Sharmistha Roy; thank you for dedicating time from your packed schedule to review this manuscript. Your insightful feedback has been crucial in refining this work.

Mr. Siddharth Mathur deserves special mention for turning the raw manuscript into a pleasant and readable form.

I am grateful to my young friends Mr. Koushik Dutta and Mr. Abdul Aziz for designing the cover.

I would also like to thank Mr Arvind Arya, who is like my elder brother—a retired banker, accomplished blogger, and published author. Your inspiration and kindness in connecting me with your publisher have been paramount. Your achievements and generosity set a sterling example.

To the one in charge of my life's support system, my lovely, gorgeous, and extraordinary life partner, Sushmita. Your unwavering support reignited my passion for cricket. Your willingness to share me—and my time—with cricket speaks volumes of your love and understanding. No words can adequately express my gratitude for your love, sacrifices, and belief.

To my sons, Ananya and Anik: Ananya, your active partnership in my ventures, both on and off the field, brings immense joy. Those precious moments of father and son playing together in the same team and occasionally against each other will forever remain etched in my heart. Anik, your quiet yet steadfast support embodies the importance of perseverance and silent strength. You are both my greatest pride and inspiration.

To everyone unnamed here who has contributed to my journey, whether directly or indirectly, your impact is acknowledged. Each of you has played a vital role in this story, and for that, I am profoundly grateful.

Introduction

Cricket has always been more than just a game. For Akhil, it was his first love, a teacher, a guide, and a mirror to life itself. Cricket became a constant companion, shaping his character and imparting invaluable lessons about resilience, leadership, gratitude, and consistency. This story is not about a hero, an extraordinary man, or a celebrated cricketer. It is about an ordinary boy's extraordinary journey—a quest to find happiness, fulfilment, and to simply be a good human being.

The story begins in the early 1980s in the timeless town of Banaras where Akhil's father, having completed his PhD at IIT Kanpur, accepted a position at Banaras Hindu University. For his father, the city represented the realisation of dreams. Little did anyone know, Banaras was destined to play an equally transformative role in Akhil's life.

In the sacred and vibrant lanes of Banaras, Akhil's love affair with cricket began. Introduced to the game at the age of five or six, he grew increasingly fascinated as the years passed. By the time he was nine or ten, he could often be found sitting patiently on the boundary line, watching older boys play, waiting for his chance to join. Those early days of observing the game instilled in him an understanding of its nuances and strategies.

Life in Banaras was a blend of discipline, joy, and celebration. After practice sessions or friendly matches, Akhil and his friends would cool off with a refreshing dip in the holy Ganga. Mother Ganga seemed to soak away the day's exhaustion, leaving them invigorated and connected to something greater than themselves. As dusk descended, they often sat on the steps of Tulsi Ghat, listening to the strains of Bismillah Khan's *riyaz* of raga Hamsadhwani drifting from Balaji Ghat. The setting sun painted the sky in hues of crimson, creating a serene yet inspiring backdrop to their youthful camaraderie.

Celebrations were simple but heartfelt. Victories on the cricket field were often followed by *chaat* outings, where they relished *golgappas* and shared laughter. Occasionally, the group indulged in *batichokha* feasts, enjoying the flavours of home-cooked delicacies. These moments were not just about food; they were an expression of gratitude for life's simple joys and the bonds of friendship.

Akhil's parents were the silent architects of his journey. His father, a university professor, was not just his first coach but also his most important mentor. In their modest front yard, he taught Akhil the basics of cricket—not just techniques but also values like discipline, hard work, and humility. His mother, a schoolteacher, was a pillar of quiet strength, ensuring he had the freedom to chase his dreams while offering comfort during setbacks. Their unwavering support laid the foundation for Akhil's ability to face challenges with courage and gratitude.

Akhil's persistence and love for the game gradually bore fruit. From being an expectant observer on the sidelines, he earned his place in the team. With time, his skills and dedication shone through, and he rose to become the captain of his college team. Leading the team was not just an achievement; it was a transformative experience. It taught him that leadership was more than strategy and decision-making—it was about empathy, accountability, and inspiring others to work towards a shared goal.

As a captain, Akhil learnt the importance of gratitude—not just for victories but for the journey itself. He realised that each member of the team, regardless of their role, contributed to its success. This perspective shaped his leadership style, fostering collaboration and mutual respect. These lessons stayed with him, serving as guiding principles in life.

Cricket also taught Akhil the value of perseverance. Like a spin bowler facing the onslaught of an aggressive batsman, he learnt to stay consistent, adapt his approach, and remain calm under pressure. Every delivery bowled, every run scored, and every setback faced became a metaphor for life's challenges. The game taught him to confront adversity with resilience and to find strength in consistency.

This book weaves Akhil's journey with the lessons cricket taught him. From a shy boy waiting for his turn on the sidelines to a leader guiding his team with integrity and grace, Akhil's story captures the transformative power of the game. The narrative delves into moments where cricket's challenges mirrored life's adversities, and how the discipline and focus instilled by the game became tools for overcoming obstacles.

At the end of some chapters, short reflections distil the essence of these lessons—insights into perseverance, leadership, and gratitude. They highlight how the strategies, principles, and values rooted in cricket can be applied to life. For example, the consistency a bowler displays when trying to outwit a batsman reflects the persistence needed to navigate life's hurdles, while the gratitude a captain feels for his team echoes the importance of acknowledging others' contributions.

Whether you are a cricket lover, someone seeking inspiration, or simply looking to rediscover the values of perseverance and passion, this story will resonate with you. It may even evoke memories of your own childhood and growing-up years. It serves as a reminder that happiness is not found solely in grand achievements but in the quiet, consistent pursuit of one's passions and the moments of joy shared with others.

Through Akhil's journey, we will discover that life's greatest lessons are often taught in the simplest of ways—one ball, one match, and one heartfelt moment at a time.

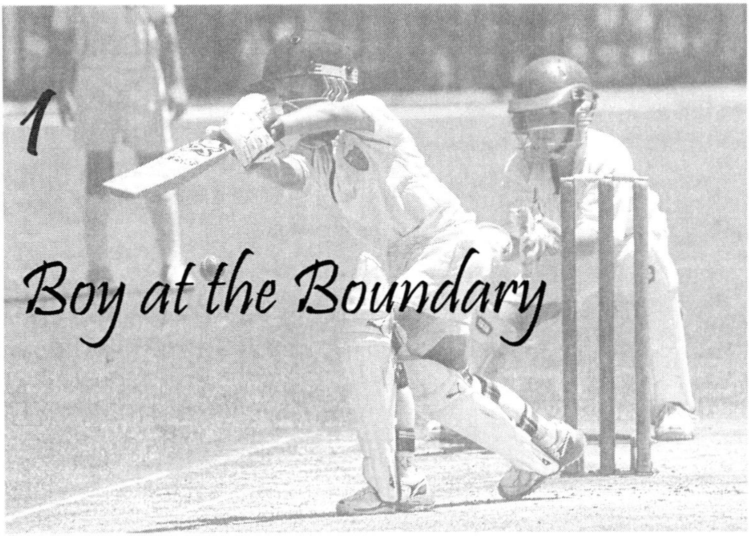

1
Boy at the Boundary

IT ALL STARTED in the early 1980s in the timeless and vivacious town of Banaras. The sacred town, perched on the Trishul of Shiva, hummed with the melodies of temple bells, the chanting of priests, and the ceaseless chatter of its narrow, bustling lanes. Amidst this enchanting chaos, a young boy named Akhilbandhu, lovingly called Akhil, began to unravel his love for cricket. With a slender frame, average height, and an earnest demeanour, Akhil seemed unremarkable to the casual observer. Yet within him burned an indomitable passion—a fervour sparked by the simplest of beginnings and nurtured by the deep-rooted traditions of a city where even the mundane held a spiritual resonance.

Akhil's journey into the world of cricket started in the quiet quarters of IIT Kanpur where his father, a revered teacher at Banaras Hindu University, was pursuing a research fellowship. Akhil's father wasn't a professional cricketer, but his enthusiasm for the sport was contagious.

It was during these formative years that the seeds of Akhil's devotion to cricket were sown.

In their modest front yard, Akhil and his father shared countless hours playing with a simple wooden bat and a mix of tennis and rubber balls.

His father, ever patient and nurturing, imparted wisdom with each toss of the ball.

"Don't just swing blindly," he'd say, tossing the ball underhanded. "Keep your eyes on it. Understand its pace and bounce. Only then decide your shot."

Sometimes, when Akhil tried his hand at bowling, his father's instructions were equally clear and encouraging: "Look at me, Akhil. Focus on dropping the ball in the same spot. Bowl straight."

These sessions were far more than mere playtime. They were lessons in patience, focus, and rhythm. The small courtyard, lined with potted plants, became Akhil's first cricket ground where his dreams took their earliest shape. Beyond the physical game, his father encouraged Akhil to nurture his mind. One day, he gifted him two books: *Sunny Days* by Sunil Gavaskar and *The Runs and Ruins*, and many more followed in times to come.

"These aren't just stories," his father explained. "They're lessons in perseverance, strategy, and the spirit of never giving up."

Akhil devoured the pages, immersing himself in tales of Gavaskar's battles against fiery bowlers and the artistry of a perfectly timed cover drive. Through these books, cricket transformed from a casual hobby to a profound passion—a devotion that shaped his every waking thought.

In those days cricket's rhythm was defined by the five-day Test matches, with a rest day after the third. The slow, deliberate ebb and flow of the game fascinated Akhil.

Whenever India played, the crackle of the family radio brought their household to life. Commentators like John Arlott, Tony Cozier, Sushil Doshi, and Narottam Puri painted vivid images with their words.

"Listen to how they describe the game," his father would urge. "Every ball has a story, Akhil. Every stroke has rhythm. Learn to hear it, and you'll understand the soul of cricket."

Akhil absorbed their commentary, imagining lush green fields, roaring crowds, and the intricate dance of bowlers and batsmen. Each broadcast became a masterclass, weaving cricket and storytelling into the fabric of his dreams.

By the time he was 14, Akhil's passion had outgrown the confines of his home. He began playing with neighbourhood *mohalla* teams on open grounds. The matches were raw and exhilarating, governed by improvised rules and scarce resources. Teams pooled money to buy a leather ball which was expected to last the entire game, and shared worn-out pads tied with ropes or handkerchiefs. Gloves were a rarity, and batsmen often relied on a single pad to protect their front leg.

Akhil would cycle miles with team kits precariously balanced on his carrier, his heart racing with anticipation. Despite his frail frame, he thrived in this unstructured environment. His enthusiasm and natural leadership drew not only younger boys but also a few girls into the game. The name 'Akhilbandhu' became more than a personal identifier; it became a symbol of unity and resilience.

Behind the scenes, Akhil's parents were his steadfast pillars of support. Though not affluent, they never let him feel the weight of their financial constraints. His mother, a dedicated schoolteacher, played a quiet yet crucial role.

She stitched his flannel whites, knitted sweaters with borders in cricketing colours, and repaired the team's pads and gloves. Before matches, she chalked his Bata Skeeter shoes to a pristine white and tended to his injuries with unwavering care.

The cricket whites his mother lovingly made were Akhil's most cherished possessions. He dreamed of owning his own bat and other equipment one day, but his parents' values taught him an important lesson: prove yourself worthy of each piece before asking for it. This belief grounded Akhil, filling him with gratitude and determination.

When friends weren't available to play, Akhil turned to the wall of their courtyard. It became his steadfast partner in practice, never tiring or complaining. He honed his bowling accuracy, perfected his catching, and refined his batting by throwing the ball against the wall and playing it on its return. Hours melted away in this solitary ritual, deepening his connection with the game.

Two moments left an indelible mark on Akhil. The first was June 25, 1983, when Kapil Dev and his team lifted the Prudential World Cup at Lord's. The second came on March 10, 1985, when India triumphed in the Benson & Hedges World Championship in Australia and the whole team rode around the ground in Ravi Shastri's Audi. These victories ignited Akhil's dreams, fuelling his determination to carve out his own place in cricket.

Sometime in 1985, his father brought home a colour television, a luxury at the time. The vibrant images of cricket matches on the screen accelerated Akhil's learning. He studied the techniques of batsmen, the actions of bowlers, and the strategies of captains with an unrelenting focus.

His father remained his mentor, guiding him through the intricacies of the sport.

Yet, Akhil's journey wasn't without its challenges. His slight build and average height often led local club teams to overlook him in favour of sturdier players. Undeterred, Akhil carried his cricket whites in his school bag, ready for any opportunity. He stationed himself at the boundaries during club matches, catching stray sixes and retrieving balls hit for fours. While others ignored him, Akhil observed every detail—field placements, bowler strategies, and batsmen's techniques.

Realising that glamorous, medium-pace bowling wasn't his strength, Akhil turned to off-spin. He practised tirelessly, using his newfound skill to make the most of his physical attributes. Even when sidelined, Akhil's patience remained unwavering. Like Nandi, the sacred bull waiting outside Shiva's temple, he stood quietly at the boundary, believing his time would come.

For Akhil, cricket was more than a game. It was a calling, a test of character, and a lesson in resilience. His quiet persistence and active patience became his defining traits. Oblivious to the world around him, Akhil was unknowingly shaping his character and future through every setback and triumph.

As the sun set over Banaras casting a golden glow over its ancient ghats, Akhil's journey continued. He practised, learned, and dreamed with a heart full of hope and a spirit unbroken by challenges. Somewhere within him he knew, standing at the boundary, that his story was about to begin and the cricket fields of Banaras were but the prologue to a much larger tale.

2 Crossing the Boundary

Akhil's admission to Banaras Hindu University (BHU) was like stepping through a wormhole into a worldof infinite possibilities. The sprawling campus, brimming with energy and ambition, was unlike anything he had experienced before. For someone whose cricketing life had been confined to mohalla matches and catching sixes from beyond the boundary, the sheer scale of the university's sports facilities was overwhelming. These were the same grounds at the periphery of which he had once stood, dreaming of what lay within.

Five lush cricket grounds stretched across the campus, each a haven for players perfecting their craft. The largest of them, often likened to Eden Gardens, seemed to Akhil like the Colosseum, its grandeur whispering tales of glory and grit. Tennis courts, badminton halls, hockey fields, and football pitches hummed with life and purpose. Even the scattered table tennis tables reflected the vibrant sporting culture of the university.

Yet amidst this abundance, Akhil felt like an outsider—a small club and *mohalla* player—who had never stepped onto a proper pitch. His whites, carefully folded in his college bag, remained unused. He continued standing outside the boundary, waiting patiently, his eyes scanning for a chance that might never come.

Despite the uncertainty of his cricketing journey, Akhil had begun mentoring two younger boys from his neighbourhood. They idolised him as an elder brother, and he took pride in teaching them the basics of the game. One was a promising left-arm fast bowler, and the other an agile wicketkeeper and hard-hitting batsman. Guiding them reminded Akhil of his father's teachings—gripping the bat, judging catches, refining run-ups and arm actions, and most importantly, staying disciplined in the face of setbacks.

This selfless dedication earned him respect among his peers and reflected his growing understanding of cricket as a collective pursuit, where the success of one was tied to the growth of all.

A few months into his first year, Akhil heard about the college cricket team's trial nets. This was his first brush with the infrastructure he had only dreamed of: a proper pitch, shining stumps, and professional gear. The sight of seasoned players adjusting their pads and marking their run-ups filled him with both awe and trepidation.

When his turn came, Akhil channelled all the practice and learning of his years spent waiting for this moment. He bowled with focus, his deliveries steady and accurate, surprising even some of the reputed batsmen. His fielding, honed through countless hours of catching sixes beyond the boundary, stood out as exceptional. While some fumbled under pressure, Akhil's quiet confidence shone through.

By the end of the trials, Akhil found himself among a pool of 20-25 probables for the college team. The final selection was still months away, but this was more than he had dared to hope for.

Even after being included in the practice nets, Akhil maintained his ritual of standing outside the boundary with his whites in his bag. His patience had transformed into a quiet readiness, a determination to seize any opportunity that came his way.

As weeks turned into months, Akhil began to draw attention towards him. He fielded with relentless zeal, bowled long spells, and batted steadily whenever given the chance. Though he wasn't a flamboyant stroke player, he was dependable and rarely got out, even in the nets. Senior players and selectors started recognising him not just as a hopeful aspirant but as a dependable fielder, a steady bowler, and a reliable batsman. Whenever a team needed an extra fielder, Akhil was the first name they called.

Fielding became his hallmark. While others vied for opportunities to bat or bowl, Akhil embraced his role with unshakable commitment. He dived for impossible catches, saved certain boundaries, and threw with pinpoint accuracy. His energy was infectious, earning him respect on the field.

"Why do you put so much into fielding when you know you won't bat or bowl?" someone asked him one day.

Akhil's answer was simple: "Because every opportunity is a gift. I'm grateful to be on the field, irrespective of what I'm asked to do."

This gratitude, coupled with his skill, won him the admiration of his peers who began subtly advocating for his inclusion in the team.

The day the college team was announced, Akhil's heart raced as the names were read out. He listened, hardly daring to hope, until he heard it: *Akhil*. For a moment, the world seemed to stand still. He had made it into the sixteen. What had once been a distant dream was now a tangible reality.

When he shared the news with his parents, their joy was palpable. His father, a teacher at the same university, patted him on the back with a quiet reminder: "This is just the beginning, son. You have to work harder now and prove yourself in every match. It won't be easy."

Akhil took his father's words to heart. Though he was now part of structured practice sessions with some of the best players, he continued to stand at the boundary during matches, his confidence growing with each passing day.

The morning of his first match arrived, bringing with it a mix of excitement and nervous energy. Akhil sat with another first-year player, a talented batsman almost certain to make it to the playing XI. Akhil, on the other hand, hoped merely to be the 12th man—a role that itself felt like an achievement.

Then he heard the unexpected call: "Akhil, the captain wants to see you."

Heart pounding, Akhil approached the captain who looked at him and said, "You're in the XI."

For a moment, Akhil was too stunned to respond. He had spent years standing outside the boundary, and now he was about to step inside it as a player! The reality took time to sink in, but when it did, a wave of gratitude washed over him.

Clad in the spotless whites lovingly sewn by his mother, and wearing his trusted canvas shoes, Akhil walked onto the field. The boundary ropes that had once been a barrier now framed his world—a world he had worked tirelessly to enter.

The team bowled first and Akhil was placed in crucial fielding positions, demanding the best reflexes. He didn't disappoint. With every stop, every dive, and every throw, he drew applause, sometimes even from the opposing team. His performance was a testament to years of relentless practice.

When he was handed the ball, an SG branded one, he felt a rush of nerves. He had bowled with locally made or worn-out balls on makeshift pitches but never something this pristine. Calming himself, he delivered an eight-over spell that was both economical and yielded two crucial wickets. The years of bowling against his father, his young mentees, and even the unyielding wall had prepared him well for this moment.

Despite Akhil's efforts, the opposition—a formidable team with several well-known players—posted a daunting total. Yet for Akhil the match was already a personal victory.

At lunchtime, Akhil experienced another first: a real team lunch. Sitting among his teammates, sharing laughter and strategy, he felt a deep sense of belonging. It wasn't just about the game anymore—it was about being part of something larger, a collective pursuit of excellence.

As he ate, he reflected on the journey that had brought him here. From the front yard of his quarters and mohalla matches to the university grounds, from standing outside boundaries to stepping inside them, every step had been a lesson in patience, resilience, and gratitude.

Akhil's thoughts turned to those who had shaped his journey: his father, whose coaching had laid the foundation; his mother, whose quiet sacrifices had supported him; his young mentees, who had inspired him to lead; and even the seniors who had given him guidance and opportunities.

As the team prepared to bat, Akhil knew he might not get a chance to bat that day, but it didn't matter. He had already made his mark. The boundary ropes that once separated him from his dream were now a symbol of how far he had come.

Sitting quietly, a smile playing on his lips, Akhil realised that his patience and perseverance had finally paid off. Sitting in the team tent during the innings break, he knew one thing for certain: the larger game had just begun.

Insight 1

Howzat!

Catching Your Dreams

CRICKET, CATCHING, AND CAREER: THE TRILOGY OF A CRICKET, LIFE, AND CAREER COACH

In cricket, taking a catch demands precision, focus, and adaptability. Similarly, catching your dreams in life and career requires these same attributes. Here's how the art of catching parallels the pursuit of success.

- **Eyes on the Ball: Vision and Focus**

A fielder's unbroken focus on the ball mirrors the importance of maintaining unwavering attention on your goals. Distractions can derail even the most ambitious plans, but clarity of vision ensures progress. Regularly remind yourself of your Dream Goal and prioritise tasks that align with it.

- **Judging the Flight Path: Strategic Planning**
Just as a fielder analyses the ball's trajectory, strategising your career requires anticipating changes in market trends, technology, and opportunities. Invest time in creating a roadmap that accounts for external influences, helping you pivot when necessary while staying on course.

- **Getting in Position: Preparation and Adaptability**
Reaching the ball requires swift, calculated movement, akin to the need for acquiring skills, building experience, and adapting to new challenges. Success favours the prepared and those ready to embrace change.

- **Cupping the Fingers: Creating the Right Structure**
A solid catch requires a strong foundation. Build support systems, routines, and processes that nurture growth. Surround yourself with mentors, peers, and collaborators who elevate you.

- **Hands High, In Front of Eyes: Active Engagement**
Proactivity is key to visibility and influence in your field. Take ownership of projects, seek leadership roles, and remain engaged in your industry.

- **The Pull-Back: Securing Success**
Catching the ball securely represents consolidating wins. Celebrate achievements while using them as stepping stones for greater impact. Protect your gains by continuing to grow and innovate.

• **The Safe Catch: Sustaining Success**
Holding the ball firmly symbolises the effort needed to maintain success. Lifelong learning, adaptability, and strong relationships are essential to leaving a lasting legacy.

Life and Career Coaching Techniques

1. **Goal Visualisation**: Encourage clients to envision their Dream Goal clearly and create a vision board to stay inspired.
2. **Action Plan Development**: Help them craft a step-by-step plan aligned with their goals and values.
3. **SWOT Analysis**: Facilitate self-awareness by identifying their strengths, weaknesses, opportunities, and threats.
4. **Scenario Planning**: Simulate external challenges (like market shifts) to prepare them for real-world uncertainties.
5. **Growth Mindset Coaching**: Foster resilience and adaptability to handle setbacks effectively.
6. **Accountability Partnerships**: Pair them with mentors or accountability partners to keep them motivated.
7. **Reflective Practices**: Encourage journaling and regular reviews to track progress and recalibrate strategies.

3

The Unexpected Opening

THE COLLEGE CRICKET ground was abuzz with anticipation. Post-lunch, the atmosphere was tense. The afternoon sun bore down on the field, reflecting off the sprawling cricket ground. Akhil's team sat in the shade of the pavilion, the mood tense but focused. The target they were chasing was daunting, a mammoth score built by the opposition's seasoned batsmen.

Akhil, still riding the high of his debut performance as a bowler and fielder, was sure he wouldn't be required to bat anytime soon. Feeling unnoticed and dispensable, he slipped away toward a cart selling *ganne ka ras* (sugarcane juice), a refreshing favourite in scorching Banarasi afternoons.

Akhil had always been the quintessential cricket enthusiast—the one who collected stray balls, helped set up the pitch, and was more comfortable fielding than batting. His love for the game was undeniable, but his batting skills, good enough for mohalla matches, were, at best, rudimentary. He was content being the team's utility player—a decent fielder, a steady bowler, but certainly not a batsman. Akhil had just taken his second sip of the cool, sweet juice when a sharp call jolted him.

"Akhil! Come here fast!"

His first instinct was confusion and, the second, pure terror.

"Pad up. You're opening the batting," the captain declared, his tone leaving no room for negotiation.

Akhil's world spun. Opening? Him? The boy who had spent countless matches watching from the boundary, collecting balls, and dreaming of a moment in the spotlight? The same boy who had practised defensive shots against his father's gentle throws, who had batted wearing full batting gear only in the practice nets once in a while, who knew more about watching the ball than hitting it?

"I... I won't be able to manage, *Bhaiyya*," he stammered, his voice a mix of fear and disbelief.

The captain's response was swift and decisive. "Just pad up. Do you think you know more about yourself than me?"

The air of finality in his words silenced Akhil's protests. His hands trembled slightly as he walked toward the gear pile. His heart raced, not just from nerves but also from a growing sense of disbelief. Was this actually happening?

Every piece of equipment, except the white flannels sewn by his Maa, felt foreign to Akhil, as if he were donning armour for the first time: the pair of pads, a pair of batting gloves, the thigh guard, an abdomen guard, and the helmet, whose visor cast a shadow over his already anxious vision. For someone used to only the front pad and left-hand batting gloves as a right-hand batsman in mohalla matches, suiting up with a full kit in a proper competitive match was a transformation beyond comprehension.

His senior opening partner's words were a lifeline. "Stay confident. You will manage."

He walked onto the pitch, gripping a weapon of his dreams—a Club Class Symonds Tusker bat lent by one of his senior teammates. The field settings, the count of fielders, the intimidating bowler at the top of his run-up—everything seemed designed to test his resolve.

The journey from the boundary ropes to the pitch felt surreal, almost scary. In that moment, a montage of lessons flashed through his mind: his father's patient teachings in their small front yard, seniors explaining the nuances of facing fast bowling, countless hours of watching professional matches, and the importance of watching the ball, maintaining a straight bat, and putting a price on his wicket.

He took a leg stump guard, a balanced stance that suggested more hope than confidence. The bowler's run-up was poetry in motion—rhythmic, powerful, intimidating. As the ball left the bowler's hand, time seemed to slow down. Akhil's mind raced through everything he had learned.

The ball whizzed past him before he could understand and thudded in the keeper's gloves. A miss, but he survived.

His partner, standing at the other end called out, "Take a breath. You're fine. Watch the ball."

Akhil nodded, retreating toward the leg umpire to regain his composure. He planted his bat into the ground, adjusted his helmet, and reminded himself of his father's words: "Always respect the bowler, but never let fear dictate your shot."

With every passing ball, Akhil's nerves eased. His defensive strokes gained confidence, and he even managed a couple of well-placed singles. His opening partner took the lead in scoring runs at a brisk pace and hitting boundaries, but Akhil's job was clear: stay at the crease.

The bowler changed, and spin was introduced. Even though he was a spinner himself, this was Akhil's discomfort zone. Unlike pace bowling, where he could use the bowler's pace to time the ball, the spinner had to be hit with some power, which Akhil lacked. He adjusted his stance, moving his back leg six inches inside the crease and playing for singles to rotate the strike as soon as possible. Akhil's confidence grew. He wasn't flashy, but he was steady. He rotated the strike, respected good deliveries, and played with a determination that caught the attention of everyone watching.

By the time he fell as the third wicket, Akhil had scored quite a slow but steady 30 runs. Modest in context, but every single run was earned through grit and focus. As he walked back to the pavilion, the applause from his teammates felt like validation. He had exceeded even his expectations. The captain said, "Well played, and next time, trust me!"

Later that evening, reflecting on his innings, Akhil understood that the match wasn't just about his performance. It had been a test of character, patience, and adaptability.

The next match was some days away.

Even after having played his first real competitive match, Akhil kept returning to the boundary line, the place where his journey had begun. It wasn't just about respect for the habit and nostalgia now but also about learning. He observed the rival teams keenly, studying their strategies and analysing the bowlers' variations and the batsmen's techniques of playing spin and pace.

Akhil stood at the boundary, the bag with his whites slung across his shoulders. The sun cast long shadows over the lush ground as a match between two rival college teams played out in front of him. The rhythmic clatter of the willow on the leather, the shouts of fielders, and the occasional cheer from a small crowd filled the air.

A towering six soared high into the sky, the ball spinning toward him. Akhil moved swiftly, tracking its arc, his hands steady and sure. With a precise motion, he caught the ball cleanly and threw it back to the wicketkeeper in one fluid movement. The throw landed in the keeper's gloves, after a well-measured drop, with a satisfying thud.

Some onlookers clapped, and a few players glanced his way with approving nods. Akhil gave a small smile and resumed his watchful stance.

The boundary ropes, once a place of yearning and waiting, now felt like a vantage point. His patience, a quality that had defined him for so long, remained, but it had evolved. It was no longer the quiet, uncertain patience of a boy waiting for a chance. It was now active and confident—a readiness for the next opportunity, whenever it might come.

As the match progressed, Akhil's mind flickered between the present and his future. He had tasted the thrill of playing, of contributing to a team effort, and of being pushed beyond his comfort zone by his captain. He had also experienced the weight of challenges and the joy of small victories.

For now, he was content to stand where he was, watching and learning. But deep down, he knew the boundary line wasn't his destination—it was just a step on his journey. With each passing day, Akhil grew more certain: the game of cricket had not just become a part of his life—it had become the teacher, the test, and the inspiration that would guide him for years to come.

4 The Time Out

THE COLLEGE CRICKET season ended on a subdued note. Akhil had participated in all three matches, contributing with steady bowling, excellent fielding, and modest batting performances. Despite their best efforts, the team lost each game and was knocked out of the tournament. Although Akhil's performances made him noticeable, he remained unsure about securing his place in the team the following year, especially with established players expected to return.

With the season over, Akhil's attention turned towards his academics and regular practice with his mohalla team. Access to the university's sports facilities also allowed him to explore other sports including badminton, hockey, and table tennis, helping him stay sharp and competitive. Among his mohalla mentees, Mannu—a fearless wicketkeeper and batsman—stood out. Together, Akhil and Mannu formed a formidable opening pair in local matches, and watching Mannu's evolution gave Akhil immense satisfaction.

Yet, life off the field wasn't as fulfilling. Akhil's newfound college freedom and overindulgence in multiple sports took a toll on his studies. He failed in two mathematics papers—not due to a lack of ability but from misplaced priorities. Though he advanced to his second year, the burden of those two back papers loomed over him, threatening his eligibility for the following year.

His father, a staunch supporter of his cricket dreams, was firm this time. "No more cricket until your grades improve," he declared. Akhil was heartbroken but couldn't argue. He knew he had to regain focus.

For months, Akhil stayed away from full-fledged cricket practice, dedicating himself to academics under his father's watchful eye. However, cricket never left his life entirely. He practised alone in the backyard, read books on cricket, and watched matches on television. He studied the techniques of legendary players like Sunil Gavaskar, Dilip Vengsarkar, and Viv Richards, analysing the bowling of greats such as John Embury, Tim May, and Shivlal Yadav. His father, once his mentor on the field, often joined these discussions offering valuable insights.

As the Banarasi winter set in, Akhil's longing for the game deepened. His neatly folded cricket whites and sweaters remained untouched in the almirah. Evenings found him quietly standing by the college cricket ground, watching his teammates practise. When friends urged him to join, he would sigh and say, "*Baba ne mana kiya hai.*" It was a humbling time, teaching him patience and discipline.

Slowly, his efforts paid off. Improved grades pleased his father who finally relented. "You can go back to practice, but only after classes. And be home before the streetlights come on," he said. Those words were like music to Akhil's ears. He retrieved his cricket whites from the almirah with renewed purpose and returned to the nets.

This comeback was marked by two significant moments. First, his mother, a quiet but constant pillar of support, gifted him an English willow bat—a basic Symonds model—and a new pair of batting gloves. For Akhil, they were treasures. He knew it was not easy for her to gather the resources to buy these, and he vowed to honour her gesture with his performance. Second, he began observing the game from a new perspective. No longer just an expectant player, he positioned himself strategically outside the boundary—behind the wicketkeeper to study bowlers' arm actions, or at square leg to observe batsmen's footwork. His understanding of the game deepened.

Unbeknownst to him, another observer had taken notice. Jitender Singh, the team's senior-most player and a seasoned all-rounder, had been quietly watching Akhil. Known as '*Jitender Bhaiyya*' among teammates, he had recently returned from club cricket assignments and was yet to join team practices.

In the nets, Akhil faced fresh challenges. Seniors pushed him to bat against pace bowlers with the new ball. While he wasn't a flashy batsman or big hitter, he had a knack for protecting his wicket and rotating the strike. His unassuming but effective style caught everyone's attention. Slowly, he realised he was being groomed to open the innings for the team—a prospect that thrilled and intimidated him. Determined to rise to the challenge, Akhil found solace in the unwavering support of his teammates, especially the seniors.

The return to cricket also saw Akhil's mohalla leagues take a backseat. Yet, he remained committed to mentoring young players like Mannu, who had now become a sought-after player for inter-mohalla matches. Watching Mannu excel filled Akhil with pride, a reminder of cricket's ability to build connections and inspire.

Weeks turned into months, and Akhil's confidence grew. He embraced his new role as an opener, blending patience with calculated aggression. His ability to handle the new ball and score brisk singles and doubles became his hallmark. Jitender Bhaiya, now fully integrated into practice sessions, took Akhil under his wing, offering invaluable advice on technique and temperament.

The white flannels, once confined to the almirah, were now back in action, bearing the dust and sweat of long practice sessions. Cricket had reclaimed its place in Akhil's life, but this time, he balanced it with academic responsibilities and a broader perspective on the game.

On weekends, he continued visiting his mohalla matches. He stood by the boundary, offering tips, observing, and sometimes fielding when needed. His presence was no longer that of a wistful spectator but of a mentor and learner. A towering six hit his way would see him move swiftly to catch it cleanly, drawing approving nods and claps from onlookers.

Akhil's journey was far from over. The challenges of balancing cricket, academics, and personal growth had shaped him into a more disciplined and determined individual. With every passing day, he grew surer of one thing: cricket wasn't just a passion it was his love, inspiration and motivation. And while the boundary ropes still held a special place in his heart, they were no longer his destination. They were merely a step in his ever-evolving journey.

For Akhil, the game of cricket had become more than just a sport. It was a reflection of life—demanding resilience, adaptability, and unwavering commitment. As he stood at the crossroads of ambition and responsibility, he knew the lessons he'd learned on and off the field would guide him for years to come.

Howzat!

Precision over Power: A Spinner's Leadership Tips

Leadership for mid-career professionals is often misinterpreted as an aggressive push for the top. But true, lasting success comes from strategic consistency, adaptability, and resilience. Like a spinner on the cricket field, mid-career leaders can achieve remarkable results by mastering subtlety over spectacle. Here's how the art of spin bowling translates into effective leadership.

The Spinner's Leadership Blueprint

- **Short, Measured Run-Up: Start with Focus, Not Fury**

A spinner's run-up is deliberate, designed to conserve energy while building just enough momentum to deliver with precision.

> ➢ *Tip:* As a mid-career leader, there's no need to prove yourself through constant hustle. Channel your energy into high-impact areas and let your expertise and preparation do the talking. Focus on strategic priorities to make your efforts count.

- **Smooth Action: Execute with Finesse**

A spinner's delivery is fluid, marked by simplicity and grace rather than force.

> ➢ *Tip:* Simplify your leadership style. Communicate clearly, avoid micromanaging, and empower your team through effective delegation. Smooth, thoughtful execution builds trust and confidence within your team.

- **Pinpoint Accuracy: Consistency is Key**

Spinners thrive on accuracy, landing the ball repeatedly on the same spot to build pressure over time.

> ➢ *Tip:* Consistency in leadership builds reliability. By meeting deadlines, maintaining quality, and upholding promises, you create a stable environment where your team can thrive.

- **Subtle Variations: Adapt Without Drama**

Spinners use slight changes in spin, line, or length to keep batsmen guessing.

> ➢ *Tip:* Adopt subtle but deliberate shifts in strategy to adapt to evolving challenges. This keeps your

leadership dynamic without overwhelming your team with constant changes.

- **Active Patience: Results Take Time**

A spinner trusts their process, bowling ball after ball with persistence, knowing success is built over time.

> ➢ *Tip:* Cultivate active patience. Focus on long-term goals rather than instant gratification, staying committed to your vision while allowing results to unfold naturally.

- **Resilience and Conservation: The Long Game**

Spinners save their energy, ensuring they can sustain their performance across long spells.

> ➢ *Tip:* Avoid burnout by pacing yourself and empowering your team. Resilience is about knowing when to step back, delegate, and recharge. Sustainable leadership ensures you can lead effectively over the long haul.

Career and Life Coaching Techniques

1. **Energy Management Training**: Teach leaders to identify their energy highs and lows, helping them allocate effort where it matters most.
2. **Strategic Goal Alignment**: Guide them in aligning personal and organisational goals to maintain clarity and focus.
3. **Mindfulness Practices**: Introduce techniques like meditation or reflection to help leaders stay calm and focused under pressure.

4. **Scenario Simulation**: Role-play potential challenges to build adaptability and quick decision-making skills.
5. **Feedback Loops**: Encourage regular feedback from peers and team members to refine leadership strategies.
6. **Empowerment Workshops**: Train leaders to delegate effectively, fostering trust and team growth.
7. **Time Auditing**: Help them assess where their time is spent and reallocate it toward high-impact activities.
8. **Resilience Building Exercises**: Incorporate practices like journaling, gratitude, and stress management to build mental toughness.

5

The Turning Point

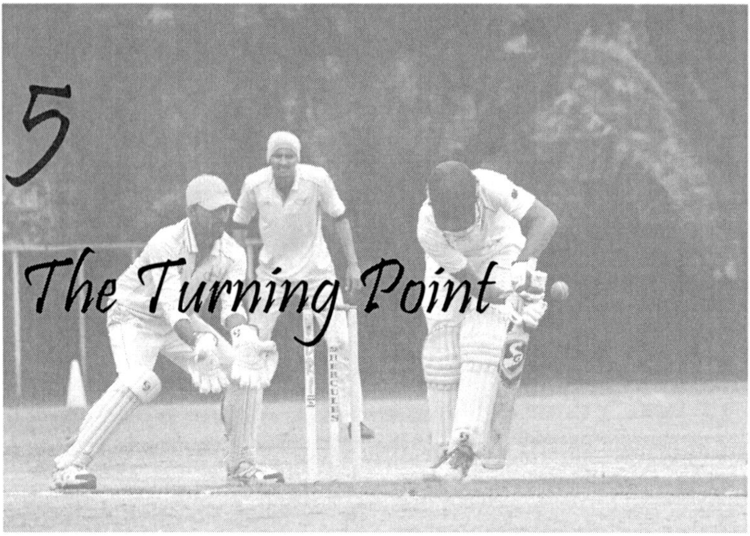

THE SECOND YEAR of B.Sc. began with a fresh sense of responsibility for Akhil. The stern but well-meaning time-out imposed by his father had left its mark. While cricket still dominated his thoughts, he had learned to strike a better balance, allocating more attention to his studies. Yet, unbeknownst to him, cricket was quietly teaching him lessons that would shape not only his game but also his very identity.

The cricket field was abuzz with new energy. Jitender Bhaiyya, a senior player and mentor to many, had returned from his professional commitments, bringing along other seasoned players. Their presence transformed the dynamics of practice sessions entirely. Gone were the days of relaxed drills and casual camaraderie. The field now resembled a professional training camp with a strict regimen and unyielding discipline.

Latecomers were relegated to fielding duty without a chance to bat or bowl. Fielding sessions, mandatory for everyone, were gruelling. Dropped catches were unacceptable—players had to persist until they successfully caught five consecutive balls, even if it took twenty attempts. Batsmen dismissed on their first ball of practice were done for the day. Bowlers who bowled no-balls had to run laps equivalent to their offences.

The nets were no longer just practice grounds; they were arenas of simulation, designed to recreate the pressure and intensity of actual matches.

Among the juniors, Akhil found himself singled out for especially challenging drills. Long spells of fielding practice and extended bowling stints became his routine. While fielding was his strength, the endless repetition sometimes wore him down.

Bhaiyya, batting karna hai thoda.... I'd like to bat a little, he ventured one day, his voice tinged with exhaustion.

Milega, Jitender replied firmly. *Abhi jo bol raha hoon karo...* You'll get your chance; do what I'm asking now.

Though he obeyed, Akhil couldn't help but feel a pang of frustration. His dreams of becoming a regular opening batsman seemed to be slipping away. The lack of consistent opportunities to face the new ball dampened his spirits. He began to doubt whether he would even make the playing XI this season.

What Akhil didn't realise was that his seniors were preparing him for something far greater. The relentless drills and rigorous routines were not punishment but preparation. He was being shaped into a player capable of thriving under the harshest conditions—a role that demanded resilience, adaptability, and responsibility.

The schedule for the inter-college tournament was announced, sparking excitement and nervous anticipation.

Akhil's college was placed in a challenging group, drawing strong opponents.

When the squad of sixteen was declared, Akhil was relieved to find his name on the list. He had expected little more, content to contribute in practice and perhaps get a chance in less crucial games.

Practice matches followed, and Akhil delivered steady performances. His bowling was reliable, his fielding sharp, and his catching consistent. Yet, the feedback he received from his seniors was understated.

*Thik hi hai...*It's okay, they would say, their tone revealing neither disappointment nor praise.

Determined to make a stronger impression, Akhil pushed himself harder, searching for ways to stand out.

The first match of the tournament was against a modestly competitive team. To Akhil's surprise, he was named in the playing XI. The senior players took the lead, ensuring a comfortable win without breaking much sweat. Akhil bowled a tidy spell and fielded with his usual energy, but his batting wasn't required.

I played because it wasn't a strong team, Akhil reasoned, tempering his excitement.

However, as the tournament progressed, Akhil's name continued to feature in the playing XI. Match after match, he found himself trusted to deliver. Though he wasn't the star of the team, his fielding made a noticeable impact. Diving saves, boundary-line retrievals and reliable catching gave the team an edge.

Akhil soon realised that his consistent fielding was not only helping to save runs but also boosting the morale of his bowlers. The bowlers wanted him to stand at the most crucial positions, even if that meant Akhil running across the field to take his place. His presence on the field had become an asset, earning him the trust of his captain and seniors.

In a crucial match against a top-tier team, Akhil found himself in a situation that would test both his skills and his mettle. Stationed at short midwicket, he faced the challenge of fielding against one of the opposition's most formidable batsmen.

A ball was played on the front foot and lobbed into the air off the batsman's bat and pad. Akhil dived full stretch, his fingers brushing the ball, but it slipped from his grasp.

The collective gasp from his teammates was punctuated by Jitender's sharp voice. *Pakadna tha! So raha tha kya?...* You should have caught it! Were you sleeping?

The reprimand stung. Akhil felt the weight of disappointment, but before he could dwell on it, his teammates rallied to his defence.

Bhaiyya bahut kathin tha...nahi ho pata.... It was extremely difficult, almost uncatchable, one of them said.

Jitender's response was curt but revealing. *Pata hai tum se nahi hota, isiliye Akhil ko rakkha tha wahan....* Yes, I know it was difficult and none of you would have caught it. But I'm talking to Akhil—that's why I placed him there!

In that moment, there was a re-programming within Akhil. The frustration he had felt during his rigorous training was replaced by clarity. Jitender's harsh words weren't an indictment; they were a reflection of faith. His mentor expected more of him because he believed Akhil was capable of more.

Though the burden of such expectations was heavy, it ignited a sense of purpose. Akhil resolved to rise to the challenge, his energy and focus on the field reaching new heights.

The tournament unfolded with highs and lows. Akhil's team performed admirably, winning most of their matches. However, losses against stronger opponents kept them from reaching the finals.

For Akhil, the tournament was a journey of growth. His consistent performances in fielding and bowling drew attention, marking him as a player to watch. Yet he knew that the path to the top was still long and demanding.

The lesson he had learned that day on the field: Make people accountable to themselves, be their accountability partner, and they will realise their true potential and prosper.

While Akhil's cricketing journey was unfolding, another challenge loomed on the horizon—his academics. To progress to the third year of B.Sc. he needed to clear ten papers from his second year and two backlogs from his first year.

The pressure wasn't just his own; his parents had high expectations of him. His father, whose stern words had sparked his turnaround, and his Maa, whose quiet support had been his anchor, both hoped to see him succeed.

Balancing the demands of cricket and academics was no easy feat. Late-night study sessions followed gruelling practice drills, leaving Akhil perpetually exhausted. Yet, he found himself drawing strength from the discipline he had developed on the field.

As the year drew to a close, Akhil stood at a critical juncture in both his cricketing and academic journeys. The lessons he had learned on the field—resilience, responsibility, and the value of preparation—began to shape his approach to life beyond cricket.

Jitender's words echoed in his mind: *I placed you there because I believe you could do it.*

That belief, coupled with his determination, became the foundation for Akhil's growing confidence. Whether on the cricket field or in the classroom, he was learning to embrace challenges, knowing that each one was an opportunity to grow.

Though the path ahead was uncertain, one thing was clear: Akhil was no longer just a player or a student. He was becoming a person ready to face life's many boundaries—and cross them.

Akhil's second year of college cricket was a crucible of challenges and growth. Every moment was a test, from gruelling practices to unrelenting expectations. But it was through these trials that Akhil discovered his purpose in the field and beyond.

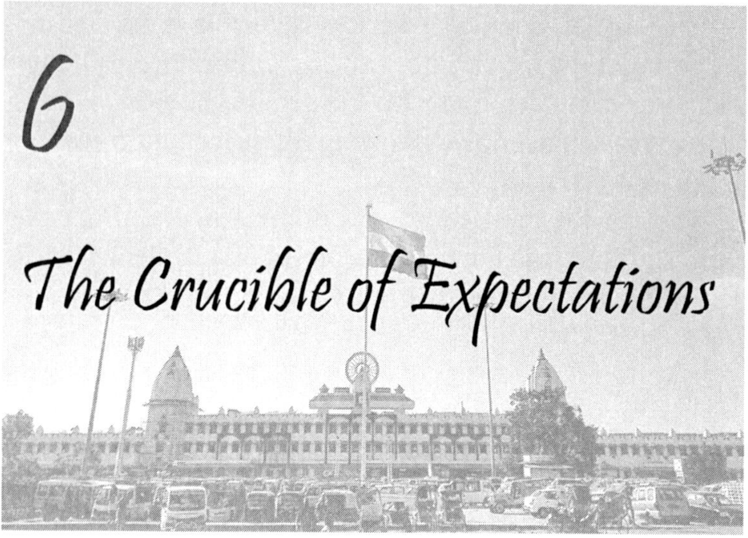

6

The Crucible of Expectations

RESULTS FOR THE B.Sc. First Year and Second Year exams were out. The queue at the mark sheet collection counter seemed unusually long, and Akhil's nerves were getting the better of him. As he neared the window, he couldn't shake the gnawing feeling in his chest. For weeks, his mind had been preoccupied with the same relentless questions: "Did I study enough? Were my answers good enough? Will I make it to the third year?"

The stakes couldn't have been higher—he had flunked two out of ten papers last year and now needed to clear all twelve to move to the final year. It felt like being bowled out on a placid track by a medium-pacer and then being thrust into an opening role against the fastest bowlers on a green, bouncy wicket.

When it was finally his turn, with a shaky hand, Akhil signed the acknowledgement sheet and was handed two mark sheets—one for B.Sc. First Year and another for the Second Year. The first hurdle was clearing the two backlogs from the First Year. He unfolded the marksheet, eyes darting straight to the critical row: "Pass/Promoted/ Failed."

'PASSED'

The word sent a wave of relief coursing through him. He exhaled deeply, a tension he hadn't realised he was holding, leaving his body. Two down; ten more to go.

The real test, though, was the B.Sc. Second Year's mark sheet. He hesitated before opening it, his heart pounding so loudly he could barely hear the bustling noises around him. When he finally summoned the courage to look, there it was:

'Passed and promoted to B.Sc. Third Year.'

It felt like hitting the winning boundary in the final over. Relief, joy, and gratitude washed over him. Though he had fallen short of a First Class by a whisker, he couldn't have asked for more at this moment.

At home, Akhil shared the news with his parents. "I passed!" he exclaimed. His parents smiled; their unwavering faith in him evident.

"I'll do better next year," Akhil vowed. "I'll get a First Class."

His parents nodded in quiet support. They had always believed in his ability, even when he doubted himself.

However, his subpar performance in mathematics meant he had to take Chemistry as his honours subject instead of his preferred choice, Physics. It wasn't ideal but cricket had taught him the importance of adapting to unexpected situations. Just as a batsman adjusts to a tricky pitch, Akhil resolved to approach this challenge head-on.

Unbeknown to Akhil, Chemistry was a cog in the wheel of God's design for him. Little did he know that Chemistry, in times to come, would create a concoction of experiences that he had only envisioned in his wildest fantasies.

Life soon settled into a rhythm. With fewer subjects to focus on, Akhil devoted more time to his studies while still indulging in sports. Cricket remained his first love, though badminton, table tennis, tennis, and hockey filled the gaps before the college cricket season began.

Akhil was determined to achieve a First Class in his final year but his resolve didn't stop him from occasionally skipping classes to spend time at the cricket ground. He thrived on the camaraderie with his teammates and the sense of purpose that cricket gave him.

As the cricket season began, the university campus buzzed with excitement. The prestigious Rohinton Baria Inter-University Trophy was to be held at Banaras Hindu University (BHU), followed by the Vizzy Trophy.

For senior players, these tournaments were golden opportunities to shine and potentially secure spots in the state or national teams. The excitement was palpable, and even players like Akhil, who weren't in contention for selection, felt the ripple effect.

Akhil approached practice with renewed energy. His consistent performances earned him invitations to bowl at the nets for senior batsmen, giving him the chance to refine his craft against some of the best players around. He began to make a name for himself as a reliable bowler with exceptional control and who could bowl long spells.

When the university team for the Rohinton Baria Trophy was announced, many of Akhil's seniors made the squad, including Jitender. Akhil felt proud of these players, who had practised alongside him.

Throughout the tournament, Akhil watched from the boundary, eagerly catching every six that came his way.

BHU played well but could not make it to the finals. Jamia Millia Islamia University took the trophy, defeating Pune University by 65 runs.

With the tournament over, attention shifted to the Vizzy Trophy. Zonal teams—East, West, North, South, and Central—arrived in BHU, with the East Zone squad featuring a couple of players from BHU.

Akhil's heart soared when he was named in a squad to play a practice match against one of the zonal teams. This was the highest level of cricket he had ever played—a three-day, two-innings match that demanded both skill and stamina.

The match was an eye-opener. Akhil bowled long, disciplined spells against top university players, troubling some with his accuracy. However, the gulf in class between him and the zonal players was evident. They played with a finesse and confidence that humbled him.

Even as a fielder, where he usually excelled, Akhil found himself feeling just above average in such elite company. It was a sobering experience but one that enriched his understanding of the game.

As the Vizzy Trophy unfolded, Akhil stood at the boundary soaking in the atmosphere. He had no expectations other than to learn and enjoy the experience. Watching the best players in action deepened his appreciation for the game.

With the Vizzy Trophy over, Akhil returned to the college nets. The inter-college tournament was cancelled that year due to the glut of cricket, leaving Akhil to channel his energy into self-improvement.

Without the presence of seniors, he practised harder, often without supervision. His drive wasn't fuelled by the need to prove himself to others but by a personal desire to raise the bar.

Akhil understood that he might never reach the heights of the players he had bowled against during the practice match. But that didn't deter him. He was determined to be counted among the best in his circles, even if it meant standing at the boundary, waiting for his chance.

He had no illusions of fame or glory. Akhil's love for cricket wasn't about being in the limelight but about cherishing the game in all its forms—playing, watching, and learning.

He was a loyal lover of the game, finding joy and beauty in anything and everything related to it. Whether catching a six at the boundary or bowling to a seasoned batsman, Akhil approached every moment with gratitude.

With the cricket season winding down, Akhil refocused on his studies. His promise to secure a First Class remained at the forefront of his mind, and he was determined to deliver.

Cricket, however, continued to anchor him. It wasn't just a sport—it was a sanctuary and a source of unending joy.

As Akhil practised at the nets, he reflected on the lessons cricket had taught him: resilience, adaptability, and the value of patience. He didn't need to be a star to love the game.

For Akhil, standing at the boundary and giving his all—as a player or a spectator—was his way of expressing his love for the game.

Howzat!

The Master Fielder's Playbook: Career Lessons from the Inner Circle

Core Skills Mantras

- **The Jonty Rhodes Effect**: Like the legendary fielder who revolutionised the game, master the fundamentals that make you indispensable in any position.

- **The Jadeja All-Round Impact**: Just as Jadeja excels in every fielding position, develop versatility that makes you valuable across functions.
- **The Kapil Dev Moment**: Like his legendary backward-running catch, be prepared for opportunities that come from unexpected directions.
- **The Slip Cordon Symphony**: Success, like a complex slip catch, requires perfect coordination between individual excellence and team dynamics.
- **The Specialist's Paradox**: Even experts falter occasionally. Foundational skills, like fielding in cricket, ensure consistent value regardless of circumstances.
- **The Support System Theory**: Like fielders backing bowlers, foundational skills—teamwork, communication, and adaptability—enhance specialised abilities.
- **The Always-in-Play Principle**: Specialised skills shine at specific moments, but core skills like critical thinking and resilience are always relevant.
- **The Collective Impact Reality**: Individual brilliance requires collective competence to deliver results. Team success relies on everyone doing their part effectively.

The Modern Workplace Reality

In an age where AI and automation disrupt specialised roles, foundational skills are indispensable. Professionals who pair deep expertise with fundamental competencies remain adaptable and irreplaceable. Much like fielding in cricket, these basic skills are your insurance against obsolescence.

Key "Fielding Skills" for Career Success:

- **Always Relevant**: Communication, problem-solving, adaptability.
- **Universally Valuable**: Team collaboration and attention to detail.
- **Crisis-Proof**: Critical thinking, resilience, and focus under pressure.

Application Framework for Career Coaching

1. **Identify the 'Fielding Skills'**:
   - Encourage clients to pinpoint core competencies that complement their primary expertise.
   - Highlight overlooked skills that can add value to their role.

2. **Develop Systematically:**
   - Create routines to strengthen fundamental skills through workshops, simulations, or role-playing scenarios.
   - Foster opportunities to apply these skills in real-world situations, such as teamwork in cross-functional projects.
3. **Measure Impact:**
   - Track how foundational skills enhance overall performance.
   - Document instances where these skills helped navigate challenges or seize opportunities.

Life and Career Coaching Techniques

1. **Skills Audit**: Work with clients to assess their strengths and identify gaps in foundational and technical skills.
2. **Scenario Training**: Use real-life simulations to teach problem-solving, resilience, and adaptability under pressure.
3. **Storytelling for Impact**: Help clients narrate how their fundamental skills have created tangible results in their careers, building confidence and self-awareness.
4. **Goal Reframing**: Align short-term objectives with long-term skill development for sustained career relevance.

5. **Cross-Skill Development**: Encourage diversification by linking core competencies with specialised expertise.

In a world where disruption is inevitable, professionals who master both their primary expertise and essential 'fielding skills' stay ahead. By focusing on readiness, relevance, and resilience, they ensure their contributions remain valuable—just like the fielder who turns a match with one game-changing catch.

7

Promises to Keep

WITH THE CANCELLATION of college cricket matches during Akhil's final year of B.Sc., he found himself at a crossroads. Although his passion for cricket remained undiminished, he channelled more time and energy into his studies than he had in the previous two years. The goal was clear—achieving a First Class degree, as he had promised his parents. This was more than an academic milestone; it was a matter of honour and gratitude towards those who had unwaveringly supported him. Alongside this, Akhil applied for admission to the M.Sc. programme, an aspiration that carried its own challenges, given the fierce competition from students within the university and beyond.

Despite his academic focus, a sense of apprehension lingered—akin to the subtle sledging he occasionally faced on the cricket field. The delay in announcing the results only heightened his nervousness. When the day finally arrived, Akhil was among the first to collect his marksheet.

Unfolding the paper with trembling hands, he searched not for the simple reassurance of the word 'PASSED' but for evidence that his efforts had borne fruit.

The results brought relief and joy—Akhil had secured a First Class. While his marks were just shy of his personal aspirations, they were enough to fulfil his promise. His parent's pride and happiness mirrored his own sense of accomplishment. The achievement marked a symbolic transition, much like his cricketing evolution from merely surviving on the pitch to performing consistently. It also secured his admission to the M.Sc. programme, opening a new chapter in his academic life.

The M.Sc. course introduced Akhil to a diverse mix of students from different colleges, states, and cultural backgrounds. The experience felt familiar, reminiscent of the camaraderie he had experienced during inter-zonal cricket tournaments. Though naturally introverted, Akhil's time on the cricket field had instilled in him a quiet confidence. He navigated this new environment with humility, finding a sense of belonging amidst the eclectic crowd.

Among the new faces were some old acquaintances—schoolmates who had pursued other courses but were now part of the M.Sc. programme. The reunions added a layer of camaraderie to Akhil's academic pursuits. The classes themselves were rigorous, demanding a level of self-discipline that Akhil likened to executing a cricket coach's strategy. Library sessions, seminars, and laboratory work filled his days, which, while less hectic than his B.Sc. years, required sharper focus and initiative.

In the quieter interlude before the cricket season, Akhil indulged in casual tennis-ball cricket with his hostel mates—a light-hearted prelude to the more serious matches that winter would bring.

As the crisp air of winter arrived, it heralded the return of the cricket season. Akhil retrieved his whites from the wardrobe, feeling a familiar excitement. At the college nets, the pre-selection trials introduced a wave of new faces. With senior players having graduated, Akhil found himself elevated to the role of a senior player—a responsibility that both humbled and inspired him. Overseeing trials and managing practice sessions underscored the respect he had earned through years of dedication.

One evening during the trials, a tall, broad-shouldered boy arrived at the nets, his demeanour both nervous and determined. Akhil recognised him instantly—a former schoolmate and a fast-bowling all-rounder who had been a star in school cricket. Back then, Akhil's frail frame had often relegated him to the sidelines while this boy had shone brightly. Now seeing him seeking a spot on the college team felt like a poetic twist of fate.

Initially Akhil allowed himself a moment of satisfaction, recalling the perceived injustices of their school days. The boy's batting trial did not go well—he seemed out of touch and visibly anxious. As Akhil observed his dejection, a thought struck him. This was not an opportunity to settle old scores but a moment to honour the spirit of the game. Cricket, after all, was about fairness and merit, transcending personal histories.

"*Woh to basically fast bowler tha, school mein bahut accha karta tha. Bowling ka chance dete hain usko...*" Akhil suggested. (He's primarily a fast bowler; he used to do well in school. Let's give him a chance to bowl.), Akhil advocated for him to the seniors.

The boy was handed the new ball. When Akhil faced him in the nets, the bowler's pace and precision were evident, earning him a second chance in the final trials. Later, when senior players sought Akhil's opinion, asking, "*Kya karna hai tu hi bol?*" (What do you think we should do?), he replied, "*Final trials tak dekhte hain na...*" (Let's keep him till the final trials and then decide.) The boy's inclusion was secured, and Akhil felt a quiet satisfaction—not from vindication, but from being able to rise above personal biases to do what was right.

Off the field, Akhil's life took on new dimensions. His easy-going nature and reputation as a cricketer drew attention, particularly from female classmates. Some helped him with practical assignments and files when he skipped classes for matches. Occasionally, they would wave at him from the roadside boundaries, drawing amused comments from his teammates. Among these admirers, a few stood out, but Akhil took it all in stride, enjoying the light-hearted banter and camaraderie.

Another significant development was Mannu's admission to a college within the same university. Akhil had always considered Mannu a younger brother and a protégé. Now, with Mannu poised to enter college cricket, Akhil took it upon himself to attend his trials. Watching Mannu's stellar performance as a wicketkeeper-batsman filled Akhil with pride. Mannu's agility and fearless batting ensured his place in the team, and Akhil marvelled at how his mentee had grown into a player who, in many ways, surpassed him.

Though Akhil's schedule remained packed, he missed the mohalla matches that had first kindled his love for cricket. Whenever he had the chance, he would stand at the boundary to watch local teams play. The boundary, once a physical and symbolic barrier, had become a place of solace—a vantage point from which Akhil could observe, learn, and reconnect with his roots.

Cricket continued to shape Akhil's character, teaching him lessons that transcended the game itself. It was no longer just about excelling in matches but about embracing the discipline, teamwork, and resilience that cricket demanded. These values seeped into every aspect of his life, guiding him through the complexities of young adulthood.

As Akhil juggled his studies, cricket, and evolving relationships, he recognised the interconnectedness of these experiences. The boundaries between the cricket field and life blurred, each enriching the other. Cricket had taught him to adapt to challenges, cherish the journey, and find joy in the process rather than being attached solely to outcomes.

The seasons rolled on bringing new challenges and opportunities. Yet, through it all, cricket remained Akhil's anchor—a constant amidst life's ever-changing rhythms. With each passing day, his passion for the game deepened not just as a player but as a lifelong student of its lessons. Standing at the boundary or taking guard on the pitch, Akhil knew that the game he loved would continue to shape his journey in ways both profound and unexpected.

8

The Ebb

THOUGH AKHIL WAS far more focused on his studies in his first year of M.Sc. than he had been during his initial year of B.Sc., distractions seemed to multiply. Cricket, student politics, voluntary community service, street theatre, and his special friends who clamoured for his attention. The balancing act between these commitments required a delicate touch, something Akhil approached with varying degrees of success.

His parents, as always, were supportive of his endeavours, but they maintained one clear expectation: "You must bring in decent results." Akhil reassured them with his characteristic confidence, grounded more in the exceptional quality of his teachers and the education he was receiving than in his own diligence. He excelled in seminars and practicals, which further buoyed his belief that he could deliver academically.

Whenever he wasn't attending lectures or immersed in the library, Akhil was at the cricket nets or spending time with his close friends. On off days, he joined a group of five friends involved with an NGO, travelling to nearby villages to spread literacy and raise awareness against superstitions. This experience offered a refreshing perspective, even if it added to his already packed schedule.

Akhil's study habits had also evolved. He often went days without opening his textbooks at home, only to cram furiously on the eve of deadlines, fuelled by endless cups of black coffee. Though he believed he was doing reasonably well in his studies, cracks in his routine began to show. A telling sign was his occasional absence from cricket practice—a sacred ritual for him until now. The reason for these absences was a newfound special friend whose company he prioritised over his time at the nets.

Jitender, his senior and mentor on the cricket team, noticed these changes. Though visibly unimpressed he chose not to interfere as long as Akhil continued to perform well in practice sessions and matches. Life, for the most part, carried on as usual.

When the inter-college cricket tournament was announced, excitement buzzed through the team. This year's format was longer, with each team facing every other before the semi-finals. The extended structure thrilled Akhil's team management, who saw it as a chance to leverage their depth and consistency.

Akhil, now a core member of the team, was exempted from final trials; his place in the squad was assured. Though elated, he remained grounded, aware that such trust came with expectations. Unfortunately, his ex-schoolmate—the fast bowler Akhil had advocated for—didn't make the final cut, a casualty of the team's abundant pace-bowling talent. Disappointed but satisfied with his efforts, Akhil accepted the decision.

The tournament began, and Akhil's team faced relatively weaker opponents in the early rounds. The team's camaraderie was evident, with light-hearted jokes flying freely. "*Akhil ko team mein toh waise bhi rakhna hai, ladkiya na ayengi humara match dekhne,*" his teammates teased. (Akhil has to be in the team; girls will come to watch our matches.) There was some truth to their jest. During matches, a group of Akhil's female friends often cheered enthusiastically from the stands, much to his teammates' amusement.

Between innings or during breaks, Akhil occasionally wandered over to chat with them, much to Jitender's growing annoyance. While Akhil's bowling and fielding remained consistent, his batting form began to falter. He was dismissed cheaply in several matches, his lack of focus showing. Jitender, who had always set high standards, was visibly displeased.

One memorable match pitted Akhil's team against Mannu's, his younger protégé and mentee. The two arrived at the venue together, sharing a cycle ride. Before joining their respective teams' huddles, Akhil gave Mannu a reassuring pat on the back and said, "*Be yourself; you will do well.*"

Though Akhil's team won comfortably, he felt immense pride watching Mannu's composed performance with the bat and his sharp wicketkeeping skills. The victory was secondary to Akhil's joy in seeing Mannu grow into a dependable player, poised to make a mark in future seasons.

With consecutive wins under their belt, Akhil's team secured a semi-final spot. Their opponents were last year's champions, a formidable team with university and club-level players. The semi-final, scheduled on a cloudy, windy afternoon, promised a stern test.

Akhil's team won the toss and elected to bowl, capitalising on the favourable conditions. Led by Jitender, their pace attack dismantled the opposition for a paltry 70-odd runs. Though Akhil's contributions with the ball were minimal, his athletic fielding and sharp catching played a vital role.

The modest target, however, proved deceptive. The opposition's disciplined bowling unit quickly exploited the conditions, reducing Akhil's team to a precarious position. Asked to open the innings, Akhil initially held his ground but succumbed to a rash shot, edging to slip. As he trudged back to the pavilion, he muttered to Jitender, "*Bhaiyya, form thik nahi chal raha,*" (Brother, I'm not in form).

Jitender's response was characteristically stern. "*Form mein jab rahoge toh acche hi karoge. Lekin accha player banna hai toh tab bhi perform karna padega jab distractions ho,*" he said. (You'll perform well when everything's going right, but a good player contributes even amidst distractions.)

Despite Akhil's poor showing, the lower-order batsmen, led by Jitender, guided the team to victory. Jubilations erupted; the college had reached the finals after years of effort and heartbreak.

The final, against a team of budding engineers with university-level players, presented a different challenge. Though not as formidable as their semi-final opponents, they were still a force to reckon with.

On the morning of the final, Akhil touched his parents' feet to seek their blessings, a ritual he seldom missed before important matches. The ground had been transformed for the occasion with guest chairs for dignitaries, a display of trophies, and a joint lunch planned in the pavilion. The grandeur left Akhil awestruck.

But the day's excitement was tempered by personal disappointment. When Jitender announced the playing XI, Akhil's name was missing. It was the first time since joining the college team that he wasn't part of the starting line-up and that too in a final. Though hurt, he understood the decision; his recent performances hadn't justified his inclusion.

Named as the twelfth man, Akhil was instructed to remain focused and prepared to field the entire innings if needed. "Stay with the team and don't wander off," Jitender told him firmly.

As Akhil stood at the boundary, ready to step in as a substitute fielder, memories flooded back. This was the same ground where, years ago, he had waited outside the ropes, clutching his whites and dreaming of playing one day. For Akhil, the cricket ground was no less than the "*Garbh Griha*" (sanctum sanctorum) of Mahadev. He had never set foot inside the oval without bowing to touch the earth and looking skyward as if seeking divine permission to enter. This deeply ingrained tradition, born of his father's teachings and the cultural ethos of Banaras, filled him with reverence.

Now, standing inside the boundary, wearing the whites he once carried in his bag, Akhil's emotions ran high. He knew he would still be positioned near the ropes, but this time, he would be catching balls before they went for sixes, watched by others standing outside.

Overwhelmed by the moment, Akhil's eyes filled with tears. He felt an immense sense of gratitude—to the game, his parents, his seniors, and the younger players who had supported him and honed his skills. Cricket, as always, remained his sanctuary, a place that mirrored life's ebb and flow.

Akhil realised that even as a twelfth man, he was living a cherished dream. The game had given him so much, and he knew this was another beautiful moment in a long, lovely journey—one that was far from over.

Howzat!

It's Not Over Till the Last Balls Bowled: Lessons from Cricket for Life Coaches

As a seasoned cricket and life coach, I've often drawn inspiration from the cricket field's highs and lows to guide my clients through their journeys. Cricket is more than a game—it's a mirror to life, offering lessons in strategy, resilience, and the unyielding spirit needed to succeed.

Imagine a batsman facing the last ball in a limitedovers match, needing 50 runs to win. Impossible? Probably. But does that stop them from taking their stance, focusing, and swinging for the boundary? This 'last ball spirit' embodies the mindset life coaching must inspire: relentless effort, regardless of the odds.

Key Life Lessons from Cricket

- **Embracing Participation:**
In cricket, every player contributes—batsmen, bowlers, and fielders. In life, success isn't about hitting the biggest milestones but showing up daily and giving your best. Coaches must help clients appreciate the journey, not just the destination.

- **Personal Benchmarking:**
Just as a batsman strives to beat their highest score, individuals should set personal goals, track progress, and raise the bar over time. Recognising and celebrating every improvement builds momentum and confidence.

- **Celebrating Small Victories:**
Every boundary, every run counts. Similarly, life's small wins—like completing a task or overcoming a minor setback—are stepping stones to greater achievements.

- **Maximum Effort:**
Cricket teaches us to give our 100% whether defending a single run or chasing a mammoth target. Coaches should instil in clients the value of consistent effort, building routines, and staying accountable.

- **Resilience in Adversity:**

Handling defeat with grace and learning from it is cricket's hallmark. Coaches must help clients develop composure under pressure, drawing lessons from failures, and staying committed to their goals.

Practical Coaching Techniques

1. **Structured Assessment:**
    - Begin with a capability evaluation to identify strengths and growth areas.
    - Use regular reviews to track progress and refine strategies.
2. **Skills Development:**
    - Break down goals into smaller, achievable milestones.
    - Create tailored routines and feedback mechanisms to build confidence.
3. **Mental Conditioning:**
    - Teach visualisation techniques to help clients envision success.
    - Use role-playing scenarios to prepare clients for high-pressure situations.
4. **Resilience Building:**
    - Encourage reflective journaling to process setbacks and celebrate wins.
    - Develop a "next ball mindset"—focusing on the next opportunity rather than dwelling on the past.

In life, as in cricket, challenges are inevitable, but victory lies in how you respond. By playing each ball with passion, purpose, and perseverance, you don't just survive—you thrive. Coaching with the 'last ball spirit' ensures that no matter the odds, your clients stay in the game, swinging for their dreams.

9

The Redemption

ON THAT SUNNY winter morning, the crisp air and golden sunlight made it a picture-perfect day for cricket. The final match of the tournament was about to begin. Akhil's team had won the toss and elected to bat first. The excitement was palpable, as this was the culmination of weeks of effort and competition.

For the first time in five years, Akhil was not part of the playing XI. It had been a bitter pill to swallow but he had accepted the decision with grace, understanding that he still had a role to play. The finals were a momentous occasion, and Akhil was determined to contribute in any way he could. Though he wouldn't bat or bowl today, his chance to make a difference would come in the field, his area of expertise.

As the match began, Akhil's team's openers walked out to bat amidst loud cheers and applause from their teammates and spectators. The ground was buzzing with energy, with college circuit players and fans gathered to witness the clash. The finals weren't necessarily between the best two teams on paper, but the rivalry promised an engaging contest.

"Play," called the umpire, and the first ball of the match was bowled. Akhil's team started cautiously, facing a disciplined bowling attack from their opponents. The opposing team's wicketkeeper, Venkat, quickly drew attention. A prodigious talent who had represented his state at the under-19 level, Venkat's wicketkeeping was a masterclass in precision and agility. His effortless glove work and sharp reflexes behind the stumps made the batsmen hesitant to take risks against the spinners. The contest between bat and ball was intense, with Akhil's team managing to maintain a steady but slow scoring rate.

At the midway point, they had laid a decent foundation, keeping wickets intact. During the drinks break, one of the seniors announced, "*Ab thoda maarna hai...* We need to accelerate now." Post-break, the batsmen responded by adopting a more aggressive approach, but this also led to the loss of a few quick wickets.

Meanwhile, Akhil stood near the boundary, closest to the team tent, enthusiastically cheering for his teammates and retrieving balls hit for boundaries. Despite not being in the playing XI, Akhil's love for the game was evident. Cricket was his sanctuary, his true love, and he immersed himself fully in the moment. His focus occasionally drifted towards the trophies displayed nearby, imagining himself holding the winner's trophy aloft. However, with every wicket lost, his dreams wavered between the winners' and runners-up titles.

After another wicket fell and Jitendra, the team's senior-most player and Akhil's mentor, walked out to bat. As he passed Akhil, he patted him on the head and said, "*Tayyar reh, tujhe field pe match jitwana hai...* Be ready; you have to win us the match today!"

That single sentence stirred something profound within Akhil. Despite not being part of the XI, his mentor trusted him to be the match-winner. Akhil felt an overwhelming surge of responsibility and emotion. Did he deserve this faith? Could he rise to the occasion? What if he failed? Thoughts swirled in his mind, but beneath it all, a quiet determination began to take root.

Jitendra played a brilliant cameo, smashing the bowlers all around the ground, supported by the remaining batsmen. Together they posted a competitive total, not insurmountable but challenging for the opposition's strong batting line-up.

During the break, the players were introduced to the dignitaries, which included some of Akhil's current and former teachers and even a few national-level cricketers. One of his teachers joked, "*Tum yahan ho, tabhi sochun class mein attendance kam kyun hai...* Now I know why attendance was low in the class!" Akhil smiled nervously. The teacher added with a grin, "*Class bunk kiye ho, ab match jitna padega...* You've bunked classes, so now you need to win this match. *Jitendra bahut tareef kar raha tha tumhare fielding ki...* Jitendra was singing praises about your fielding." The weight of expectations grew heavier, but Akhil felt a strange mix of pride and pressure.

After a quick lunch, the team gathered for the final huddle before the second innings. It was decided that Akhil would come in as a substitute fielder shortly after the match began. Jitendra had no specific instructions, except the haunting reminder, "*You have to win the match for us today.*" Fielding was Akhil's strength, but the stakes today felt overwhelming.

As the teams took their positions Akhil waited by the boundary, butterflies in his stomach. After the first over, the weakest fielder was substituted out, and Akhil was called in. Before stepping onto the field, Akhil bent down to touch the ground and looked skywards, silently asking for divine blessings. "Will this be my day?" he wondered.

Akhil took his position, and the match progressed with a tight bowling display. The opposition's scoring rate was kept in check, and a brilliant run-out sent one of their top batsmen back to the pavilion. Akhil, now calmer, was fielding with precision. He took a straightforward catch at square leg, boosting his confidence further.

A couple more wickets fell and then came Venkat. He started cautiously but soon began to shift gears, playing elegant and aggressive strokes. Despite losing partners at the other end, Venkat kept the chase alive. The momentum seemed to be swinging in favour of the opposition.

The senior players, led by Jitendra, convened for a quick discussion. They decided to set an attacking field for Venkat and brought on an off-spinner. Jitendra signalled Akhil to move to square leg, just to the left of the umpire. On the second ball of the over, Venkat swept fiercely. The ball hurtled towards Akhil's right at lightning speed. Akhil dived full length, getting a hand to it but failing to hold on. The ball raced to the boundary.

A collective gasp echoed around the ground. Akhil's teammates were on their knees, hands on their heads. No one blamed him; reaching the ball was itself an incredible effort. But Akhil was inconsolable. Lying face down on the ground, he thought, "I've dropped the winner's trophy."

From the other side of the pitch, Jitendra's voice boomed, "*Dono haath se lena tha! Uth ab, fir ayega...* You should have tried with both hands! Get up; you'll get another chance." Akhil, still dejected, slowly rose to his feet.

In the next over, Jitendra approached Akhil and said quietly, "*Dekho tumhare papa aaye hain match dekhne. Jitna padega...* Your father has come to watch the match. We have to win it!" Akhil looked towards the gallery and spotted his father among the dignitaries. The sight of him made him a bit nervous but also filled him with renewed resolve.

As the game resumed, Venkat continued to dominate, and the target seemed increasingly achievable. When the off-spinner returned to bowl, Akhil asked Jitendra, "Should I move to the umpire's right? He's targeting that area with his sweeps." Jitendra's reply was firm: "Stand where you are". Akhil was a bit surprised.

Venkat swept the first ball for four. The tension was unbearable. Two balls later, he swept again. The ball followed a similar trajectory as the one Akhil had dropped earlier, but this time, it was farther. Akhil could just take a step to his right before he had to dive full length, both hands outstretched. The ball thudded into his palms, and he clutched it tightly as he hit the ground. The crowd erupted. Even the square-leg umpire could not believe it.

Akhil's teammates rushed towards him, lifting him off the ground in jubilation. Jitendra picked him up in his arms and ran towards the team tent as if they'd already won. The spectators gave a standing ovation, and even Venkat paused, acknowledging the brilliance of the catch.

Jitendra asked Akhil "*Ab samajh aa gaya kyun khada kiya tha tujhe wahan!...*Do you realise now why I kept you where I did!" The opposition's hopes were shattered...". The fact dawned upon Akhil that Jitendra had laid a trap for Venkat, banking on Akhil's skills and capabilities.

From there, it was only a matter of time before Akhil's team wrapped up the match.

After the final wicket fell, sealing their victory, the celebrations began. Students, teachers, and supporters flooded the ground, cheering for their college's triumph after years of waiting.

During the customary handshake, Venkat said to Akhil, "You won the match for your team, bro. That catch was out of the world!" Standing just ahead, Jitendra turned back and smiled at Akhil. That smile spoke volumes, conveying pride and acknowledgement of all the hard work that had gone into shaping Akhil's skills and temperament.

Later, Jitendra nudged Akhil, "*Papa se mile keaao...* Go meet your father before the presentation." Akhil hesitated. "*Aap bhi chalo...* You come too," he said. Together, they walked towards the gallery. Akhil's father hugged him and Jitendra, beaming with pride. "Well played," he said simply, but those words meant the world to Akhil. He longed to run to his Maa, break the news, see her beaming face, and get into her warm embrace—the biggest prize he could ever have. But that had to wait.

Walking back to the team tent, Akhil shyly asked Jitendra, "*Apne doston se mil ke aau zara...* Can I meet my friends for a while?" Jitendra smirked, "*Jao, lekin jaldi aana. Baaki sab ke liye baad mein bahut time milega...* Go, but come back quickly. You'll have plenty of time for everything else later!" Akhil blushed, his heart full of gratitude for his mentor, his team, and the game that had given him everything.

The boy at the boundary had redeemed himself. This was not just a victory for the team but a moment of personal transformation for Akhil, forged by faith, hard work, and the unwavering guidance of his mentor.

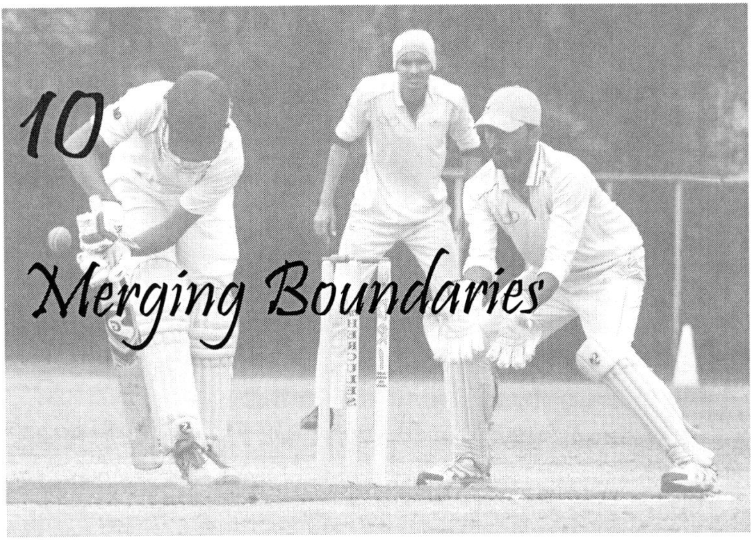

10 Merging Boundaries

THE FINAL WAS won! During the felicitation and award ceremony, amidst the many prizes distributed, Jitendra was named the Best All-rounder of the tournament. Yet, in his usual humble fashion, he politely declined the award, nominating an upcoming all-rounder from another college to receive it instead. Though not on the awardee list, Akhil was given a special mention for his exceptional fielding and catching. That acknowledgement alone sent a wave of joy through him. As Akhil held the trophy high with his teammates, he felt an indescribable elation. The certificate bearing his name and the word 'Winner' was a treasure he wouldn't trade for anything.

Back home, a small but warm celebration awaited him, hosted by his biggest supporters—his Maa and Baba. Though simple, it was the best party Akhil could ever imagine.

A joint get-together was organised for all tournament participants, along with teachers and dignitaries. Akhil, who by now was not just another player in the college circuit, was getting the attention he had earned. The college cricket circuit now knew him by name, not only for his performances but also because he was Jitendra's mentee. He enjoyed his rising stature, but amidst all the accolades and smiles, a shadow of sadness loomed. Jitendra, his mentor and guiding force, would be completing his course in two months. The thought of life without his mentor in the nets and on the team was terrifying for Akhil. "How will my cricket life be without Jitendra Bhaiyya?" he often wondered. But life, as always, demanded he move forward.

However, another piece of good news arrived—Jitendra had chosen to enrol in another course and would remain available to play for the college team. This lightened up Akhil's heart as well as others in the team, renewing their sense of unity and strength.

With his M.Sc. first-year exams approaching, Akhil resolved to avoid repeating the academic fiasco of his B.Sc. First Year. He buried himself in his studies, though his mind often wandered elsewhere. One significant distraction was his batchmate Anupama who had gradually become a constant in his life.

True to her name she was a brilliant student, pretty, graceful, a trained singer and had a voice that could enchant even the most distracted listener. Akhil found himself drawn to her in ways he couldn't fully explain. She, too, seemed to enjoy his company, though their relationship remained undefined.

Whenever Akhil wasn't in class or the library, he could be found walking beside her, their conversations flowing effortlessly. They laughed, teased, and shared quiet moments, but Akhil struggled to decipher his feelings.

He was too unsure of himself to find the courage to probe deeper.

When the exam results were announced, Akhil saw he had narrowly missed a first division. Though a stark improvement from his B.Sc. first year results, he felt a pang of disappointment. His parents encouraged him to strive harder for a first-class degree in his final year, reminding him of its importance for his future.

Anupama, on the other hand, excelled as usual, ranking among the top students. This deepened Akhil's feeling of inadequacy around her. He began to feel the gap between them—academic, social, and perhaps even emotional. Slowly, he started pulling away, avoiding her company wherever possible. Her sharp instincts noticed this change immediately.

One afternoon, she cornered him in the library. "*Kya hua hai tumhe? Kyun avoid kar rahe ho mujhe?....* What's wrong with you? Why are you avoiding me?" Akhil stammered, "*Kuch nahi... nahi toh...*Nothing, I'm not avoiding." She wasn't having it. "*Natak band karo aur normally behave karo....* Stop this drama and act like yourself." Her firm yet caring tone disarmed Akhil, and slowly, their dynamic returned to its familiar rhythm. Yet, beneath his smiles and laughter, Akhil remained uneasy. Despite enjoying her company, he couldn't shake off the thought that they were worlds apart. But his behaviour made it evident that he was not his normal self. With her female instinct, Anupama could perhaps understand what was going on inside Akhil and tried to coax him to open up, "*Kya hua hai? Kuch bologe bhi...* What is it with you? Say something!" Akhil would just say, "*Kuch toh nahi...* Nothing," and change the topic.

After classes until just before sunset when the streetlights flickered on, it was practice time for Akhil. Yet, he would sometimes steal some moments to be with Anupama. On one such chilly winter dusk, with the sky aglow in crimson hues from the setting sun, Akhil and Anupama sat together on a bench just outside the boundary of the college cricket field. Akhil, still dressed in his practice whites, gathered all his courage and stumbled through clumsy and vague words to express his admiration for her. Anupama looked at him but the silence that followed stretched awkwardly long. Saying nothing, they eventually rose and walked together in silence towards her hostel.

Though she hadn't rejected him outright, her response left Akhil in an emotional limbo. It reminded him of his early cricketing days, waiting at the edge of the boundary, longing for a chance to step onto the field. Now he stood at the edge of her heart, unsure if he would ever be let in. He buried himself in his routine, pouring his energy into cricket and studies, but her lingering presence in his thoughts was inescapable. His parents noticed his distracted demeanour but refrained from probing, offering him quiet support instead.

As the final team trials approached, the second piece of news was revealed: Akhil had been chosen to captain the college cricket team. The announcement left him momentarily stunned, but years of mentorship from Jitendra and his parents had prepared him for this moment. He embraced the role with quiet confidence, his natural charm uniting the team behind him. Akhil wasn't just the appointed leader by seniority but was unanimously accepted by his teammates. Once again, cricket became his sanctuary.

God's designs are often beyond mortals to understand, weaving paths unseen. A couple of weeks later, a mutual friend informed Akhil that Anupama wanted to meet him. Butterflies of nervousness and apprehension swirled in his stomach, but amidst them fluttered a tiny butterfly called hope. It reminded him of the same electric anticipation he had felt while waiting for the team list to be announced in his first year of college, a mix of fear and possibility that seemed to define moments of significance in his life.

When they finally met, once again on a chilly winter dusk under a crimson-painted sky, Anupama stood gracefully beneath a *saptaparni* tree, its fragrance mingling with the chilly Banaras air. She held her gaze steady on Akhil, her eyes piercing through the silence, leaving him breathless and uncertain. His heart raced wildly, convinced this was their final goodbye. But then, breaking the stillness, she spoke—unlike Akhil her voice soft yet resolute: "I will wait for you, Akhil." That moment opened another boundary he had long lingered at and finally invited him inside.

The spring was back in his steps. His cricket, captaincy, and academics remained steady and Anupama brought unspoken warmth to his life. She added layers of meaning to his days. Standing on the cricket field, commanding his team with unwavering confidence, Akhil couldn't help but reflect on how every challenge he had faced—both on and off the pitch—had led him to this point. Each setback, every victory, and all the moments in between had been preparing him for this role.

The inter-college tournament schedule was announced—a bittersweet moment. It would likely be Akhil's final tournament as part of the college team and he was determined to leave a legacy that would inspire those who followed. Jitendra, his ever-reliable mentor, would be guiding him one last time, offering wisdom laced with encouragement. For Akhil, these matches would be about more than cricket; they would be his ultimate test as a leader, a player, and a person.

As the season approached, Akhil began to notice how boundaries—both literal and emotional—started to dissolve. The lines between cricket, love, and life blurred, each feeding into the other in ways he had never imagined. The field no longer felt like just a playground but a stage where lessons of resilience, teamwork, and hope unfolded. Through it all, Akhil realised a profound truth shared by cricket, love, and life: success comes to those who dare to step forward, even when the odds are stacked against them.

With each practice session, strategy meeting, and cherished moment with Anupama, Akhil's resolve grew unshakable. The horizon ahead stretched wide and full of promise, and he felt ready to face whatever lay beyond—with a ball in his hand, a team at his back, his parents' blessings, and love in his heart. For Akhil, boundaries were no longer limits—they were invitations to step forward, to cross over, and to discover the endless possibilities waiting on the other side.

Howzat!

The Silent Guardian: Leadership Lessons from Behind the Stumps

Picture yourself on a humid day at a bustling stadium, the air heavy with anticipation. Behind the stumps, crouched and focused, you embody the silent guardian of the field. Your gloves poised for action, your mind processes every subtle movement of the batsman, every variation the bowler might employ. This is leadership at its most demanding—where success lies in mastering details often unnoticed by others.

The Wicketkeeper's Wisdom

The wicketkeeper is the team's sentinel, showcasing leadership qualities that transcend the cricket field. From local matches to international arenas, the keeper leads with vigilance, strategy, and resilience.

Core Lessons from Behind the Stumps

- **The Strategic Overview**
  - **Maintain a holistic view**: Like a keeper positioning fielders with precision, always understand the bigger picture.
  - **Anticipate situations**: Read the game before it unfolds, much like predicting a batter's intent.
  - **Balance aggression and patience**: Decisions, like a perfectly timed appeal, require both boldness and restraint.
- **The Silent Guide**
  - **Support without overshadowing**: Provide guidance while empowering others to shine.
  - **Offer valuable insights**: Act as the communication bridge between team members.
  - **Earn trust through consistency**: Build credibility by demonstrating reliability under pressure.

- **The Resilience Factor**
  - **Thrive in challenging conditions**: Whether it's physical heat or organisational pressure, adaptability is key.
  - **Recover from setbacks**: Perseverance is the hallmark of enduring leadership.
  - **Set standards for fitness and discipline**: Lead by example in maintaining physical and mental endurance.
- **Technical Excellence**
  - **Master the basics**: Whether managing spin or pace, adaptability is built on foundational skills.
  - **Embrace innovation**: Be open to evolving practices and new challenges.
  - **Mentor while learning**: Invest in the growth of others without neglecting your own development.

Leadership Applications

1. **Vigilance in Leadership**
   - Stay alert and anticipate challenges.
   - Identify opportunities before they become apparent.
   - Establish systems for proactive problem-solving.
2. **Strategic Observation**
   - Balance attention to detail with an understanding of broader dynamics.

- Foster open communication and real-time feedback.
- Adapt strategies to changing circumstances.

3. **Performance Enhancement**
   - Build resilience through structured challenges and recovery protocols.
   - Cultivate a culture of continuous improvement.
   - Create effective feedback loops to drive team growth.

Coaching Techniques

1. **The Keeper's Mindset**
   - Develop focus through mindfulness practices.
   - Strengthen decision-making under pressure with simulated challenges.
   - Build mental stamina through incremental growth exercises.
2. **Technical Excellence Programme**
   - Create assessment frameworks tailored to the environment.
   - Design drills that reflect real-world scenarios.
   - Provide individualised development plans.
3. **Leadership Development Path**
   - Enhance communication skills through interactive role-play.

- Build situational awareness with scenario-based exercises.
- Strengthen crisis management capabilities through targeted challenges.

11

The Final Final

AKHIL WAS DETERMINED to improve on his previous year's performance and began his preparation with renewed focus and dedication. Jitendra, his mentor and the former captain, reminded him of the responsibilities that came with leadership. "Now that you're captain, you must not only lead but also excel in batting," he advised. "Bowling and fielding are already your strengths. Work on your batting and take charge." Jitendra's words were etched in Akhil's mind like lines on stone. Inspired, Akhil threw himself into rigorous batting practice, spending countless hours at the nets to perfect his technique.

When the tournament began, Jitendra chose to play a supportive role, being both player and mentor, while leaving the captaincy to Akhil. This gesture of trust humbled Akhil even further, motivating him to live up to the expectations placed on him.

In the first match, Akhil delivered an impressive performance with the ball, taking a couple of wickets.

Though batting was not expected of him, he decided to step up and reacquaint himself with match situations. The game turned out to be a straightforward victory for Akhil's team, boosting their confidence as they advanced.

The second match was against a team of medical students not known for their cricketing prowess. Akhil's team was confident of an easy win. Winning the toss, Akhil opted to bat first. However, a few quick wickets left the defending champions in trouble. Akhil decided to step up, walking out with the Symonds bat his mother had lovingly purchased for him. Just as he was settling in, another wicket fell. Jitendra joined him at the crease and with his characteristic wisdom said, "Captain, you have to win this for the team." Akhil nodded and smiled, appreciating Jitendra's ability to motivate.

The duo built a solid partnership, shifting the momentum in their favour. For Akhil, the partnership was special not just for the runs they amassed but for the opportunity to bat alongside his mentor. During the mid-innings break, a teammate suggested Akhil switch to the new Sunny Tony bat. Tempted, Akhil looked to Jitendra for approval. "Stick to the bat you're comfortable with," Jitendra advised. But Akhil, eager to try the new bat, gave in to temptation.

Unfortunately, his innings ended soon after. Overconfident with the new bat, he played a loose shot and was dismissed for 70+ runs—his highest score in college cricket. Jitendra's disapproving glance said it all. Nonetheless, their team posted a formidable total and later bowled out the medical students with ease. Akhil's bowling continued to shine as he picked up two more wickets and took two spectacular catches in the slips and gully.

The next match was a different challenge altogether. They were up against one of the toughest teams, featuring several university-level players and a pace-bowling all-rounder who had represented India's under-21 team. The stakes were high as a victory would secure their place in the finals.

Three days before the match, disaster struck. Akhil injured his right thumb severely during practice, putting his participation in jeopardy. Dejected, Akhil relied on his Maa's home remedies and his family's unwavering support. Jitendra, however, was unfazed. "*Tujhe to khelna hai....* You have to play," he stated matter-of-factly. Anupama, his special one, shared her concerns but encouraged him nonetheless. His parents, understanding the significance of the match, left no stone unturned in helping him recover.

Akhil's Maa had always been his quiet pillar of strength. She was no cricket expert but her understanding of Akhil's dreams and her unwavering belief in him had shaped his journey. Every stitch of the sweater she had knitted for him, every lovingly prepared meal, and every herbal remedy she administered spoke of her motherly love. She had seen Akhil's struggles and triumphs and had always reminded him that perseverance and humility would take him far.

His father, though less expressive, had also been a constant source of encouragement. A man of few words, his pride in Akhil shone through his actions—be it in the quiet hours he spent repairing Akhil's cricket gear or the small but thoughtful gifts, like the cricket shoes he bought him after saving up for months.

On match day, with his thumb heavily strapped and painkillers dulling the ache, Akhil decided to play. Losing the toss, he was asked to bat first. To protect the team's key batsmen from the opposition's fearsome new-ball attack, Akhil chose to open the innings himself. Every ball that struck the bat jarred his injured bottom hand and caused excruciating pain but Akhil endured it, focusing solely on the team's needs. He batted resolutely for several overs before being dismissed, having done his job of shielding the team's best batsmen from the initial onslaught.

With a decent score on the board, Akhil took the field again, still battling pain. The team bowled exceptionally well, with Akhil leading from the front. Despite his injury, he bowled accurately, even earning praise from the opposition's star player for beating him multiple times. The match was finely poised and the outcome hinged on dismissing one of the opposition's set batsmen. Jitendra stepped in, asking Akhil for an over. Akhil readily agreed.

Jitendra was about to deliver a masterclass of mind games. He requested Akhil, one of the best fielders in the college circuit, to field at deep square leg, signalling a potential bouncer. As Jitendra ran in, the batsman prepared for the expected short ball. Jitendra unleashed a perfectly pitched, swinging yorker that shattered the stumps. Stunned yet impressed, the batsman nodded his head, smiled, and acknowledged Jitendra's brilliance. The dismissal broke the opposition's resistance and Akhil's team wrapped up the match with ease, securing their spot in the finals for the second consecutive year.

Celebrations followed, albeit modest. Over Banarasi *chaat* and *golgappas*, Akhil's close circle, including Anupama and his brother-like friend Mannu, revelled in the victory. A few players from the opposing team joined in, reflecting the camaraderie and shared love for cricket.

The final was a rematch against the previous year's runners-up who had bolstered their squad with new players, including a batsman fresh from playing club cricket in England. The days leading up to the final gave Akhil some time to recover, although he skipped practice to spend more moments with Anupama. The prospect of leading his team in the grand final overwhelmed Akhil with pride and gratitude. Wearing branded flannels and proper sports shoes gifted by his Maa, he still chose to don the old sweatshirt she had knitted for him, a poignant reminder of his humble beginnings.

Losing the toss, Akhil's team was asked to bowl first. The opposition attacked with a vengeance, eager to avenge their previous loss. Akhil had to bowl earlier than planned as his bowlers struggled against the onslaught. Despite the pressure, Akhil bowled with precision and guile, taking wickets at regular intervals. However, the opposition's star batsman, the one back from England, was unstoppable. Even as Akhil beat him on a few occasions, the batsman plundered runs with ease, eventually scoring a century. The opposition's total was daunting, leaving Akhil's team with an uphill battle.

Akhil's bowling performance however was nothing short of extraordinary. He claimed seven wickets, a record in college tournament, earning a standing ovation from his team and mentor. Yet, the towering target cast a shadow over his achievement.

In pursuit of the target, Akhil's team put up a spirited fight. Almost every batsman contributed, including Akhil, but they fell short by a considerable margin. The loss was disheartening but reaching the finals two years in a row was a feat in itself. For Akhil, the match carried an added poignancy as it marked the likely end of his college cricket journey.

The award ceremony was bittersweet. Akhil was in the running for the Best Bowler's trophy, competing against seasoned university and club cricketers. Though he didn't win, the respect he earned from teammates, opponents, and spectators alike was reward enough. The boy who once languished on the boundary line had grown into a captain admired by all. His unconditional love for cricket had come full circle; the game was giving back to him in ways he could never have imagined.

As the sun dipped low on the horizon that evening, Akhil stood alone at the boundary line. It was the same place he had started his journey years ago, watching others play and dreaming of his moment. Now, as he stood there, he felt a deep sense of fulfilment. The boundary was no longer a limit; it was a gateway to new opportunities, both on and off the field. He smiled, ready to step forward once more.

12

Farewell

WITH HIS LAST college cricket tournament over, Akhil felt a bittersweet ache in his chest. On one hand, he was sad that this chapter of his life had closed, yet on the other, he brimmed with pride. Mannu, his protégé, friend, and younger brother in spirit, had emerged as a star in the college cricket circuit, growing into a batsman even better than Akhil had ever been. Watching Mannu's success felt like seeing his own dreams flourish through someone else.

Taking stock of his five years in college cricket, Akhil realised his greatest pride wasn't in the best spells he bowled or the best innings he played but in contributing through the unsung art of fielding. His ability to save runs, anticipate movements, and take impossible catches often turned games around. For him, standing at backward point or patrolling the deep boundary was not a chore but a privilege. He loved the feel of the ball skimming across the ground and the sharp sting of a direct hit. Even on days when he didn't get to bowl and often didn't bat, Akhil still found immense satisfaction in contributing to the team and to the bowler's success through his fielding. Cricket, after all, wasn't just about individual glory; it was about the collective spirit where every saved run or well-placed throw could change the tide of a match.

Akhil's time on the field also gave him a profound appreciation for the bonds forged through the game. His closest friends weren't just teammates but often opponents. Cricket had a unique way of fostering respect for adversaries, teaching him that opponents weren't enemies but challengers who pushed him to be better. Some of his most cherished friendships were born out of fierce matches where mutual respect grew from shared battles under the sun. These relationships, Akhil realised, were among the most genuine and unselfish ones he had ever known. On the field, there was no room for pretence; it was a space of pure honesty where camaraderie was built on shared struggles and triumphs.

Mentors and seniors like Jitendra taught him the nuances of batting and mind games, and even opponents like Chandu's and Avanikant's (from the rival college team) masterful spin bowling inspired Akhil to push himself harder as a player. These people in their own ways contributed to his growth both on and off the field.

For the time being however Akhil knew he had to take a break from his first love, cricket, to give his undivided attention to his second love, Anupama, and of course to his studies. Anupama, true to her word and understanding Akhil's love for cricket, had waited patiently for his time. And studies—he had promised his parents and himself that he would secure a first division in his M.Sc. exam. With Anupama, an academically brilliant companion, the bar was set higher. Akhil was good at studies but often distracted; cricket had always been his priority.

When not spending time with Anupama, which rejuvenated him like nothing else, Akhil devoted himself to his family or his books. His theory papers went well and his practicals—his strength—went even better. During his last practical exam and viva voce, the external examiner, immensely impressed by Akhil's understanding, offered him an opportunity to pursue a Ph.D. under him at a renowned foreign university. To the disappointment of his teachers and parents, Akhil, who was never particularly attached to academics, dexterously declined.

When the results came out, Akhil was thrilled to see he had done well in his final year, bolstered by his performance in the practical and viva voce. His strong finish made up for his earlier lacklustre results, and he secured a first division. His parents were proud, and he was happier still to see their joy.

Anupama had enrolled for her Ph.D. programme. Meanwhile, Akhil, with his modest aspirations, chose to study computers and began searching for jobs.

A couple of years went by. After completing his computer training, Akhil joined a training institute as a trainer before transitioning into the role of a management trainee at a private sector bank. Yet, cricket was never far from his heart. Whenever he had a chance he would wander back to his old college ground and watch the boys practise, offering tips, and sometimes standing on the boundary catching sixes as effortlessly as he always did. His whites were no longer in his bag nor did he wait for a call to play, but the unadulterated joy he derived from being around cricket remained unchanged.

Anupama, meanwhile, continued to excel in her academic pursuits. They spent as much time together as possible, their relationship blossoming in quiet contentment. To those who knew them, Akhil and Anupama seemed like a perfect pair, moving steadily toward a shared future.

One evening, during a family chat, Akhil's father brought up the topic of marriage. "You have two years at most," he declared. "Either you find and finalise a girl to marry, or we will find one for you!" With Anupama by his side, Akhil simply smiled and nodded.

However, as life often does, it bowled a knockout bouncer. Anupama moved to another city for higher studies and their communication became limited to letters and occasional phone calls. More than the physical distance, it was the proximity to others and the changing circumstances that slowly began to strain their relationship. Both desperately tried to hold on to whatever they had but eventually the day came when they had to part ways. It was not because of the lack of love but due to circumstances designed by the almighty. Akhil understood the reasons—logical as they were—but accepting them was a different story.

The separation felt like an unfair decision by an umpire—a plumb LBW call given 'not out'. Disappointment hit him hard, but Akhil's cricketing journey had prepared him for these moments. Cricket had taught him that a 'no' wasn't always personal; it did not define him. Instead, it had to be understood in the context of circumstances and perspectives. It could be a dropped catch, a missed shot, or even a poor umpiring decision that had to be accepted as part of the larger design. Dwelling on them would only hinder the next delivery being bowled well. Life, Akhil realised, was no different.

As he had done countless times on the field, Akhil picked himself up, dusted off his disappointment, and prepared to move forward. He was thankful for the special girl who had shared a part of space-time in his life, and he chose gratitude, shutting out even a trace of bitterness. With the treasure troveof some lovely experiences and happy memories, he moved ahead.

Anyone suggesting him to forget Anupama and that chapter of his life would hear him reply firmly, "Why should I? She and those times are some of the best treasures of my life. I will keep them as a chapter in my book of memories, with a page marked in gold."

Akhil found solace in the lessons cricket had taught him. The game had instilled in him resilience—the ability to keep moving forward, no matter how unfair or disheartening the situation might seem.

In his quiet moments, Akhil reflected on what had transpired. He came to understand that not every boundary was meant to be crossed or conquered. Some were there to teach patience, others to offer perspective from a distance. He realised that the phase of life with Anupama did not define him; rather, it contributed to shaping him into what he is today. The experience had deepened his understanding of himself, making him more empathetic and grounded.

"It's not about the umpire's decision," he kept reminding himself, echoing lessons from the cricket field, "It's about how well you bowl the next ball."

With gratitude for the memories and lessons learned, he moved forward, ready for whatever life had in store.

Cricket remained his guiding philosophy, a constant reminder that life, like the game, was a series of innings. Each delivery was an opportunity, each setback a lesson, and each success a fleeting yet beautiful moment to cherish.

Howzat!

Captain's Diary: Two Runs That Won it All

In the high-stakes drama of a cricket match, your team needs 6 runs off the final ball to clinch victory. The last batsman, channelling pure adrenaline, launches a magnificent six into the stands. The stadium erupts, headlines write themselves, and a new hero is born. But let's rewind the tape to an easily forgotten moment—earlier that day your opener faced just one delivery, hustling for two runs before getting run out while pushing for a third.

Through conventional analytics, this brief performance might register as merely a statistical footnote. Yet, without those crucial two runs your team would have faced an insurmountable target of eight runs on the final ball. Those overlooked runs, seemingly insignificant in isolation, laid the essential groundwork for the spectacular finish that followed.

This scenario illuminates a fundamental truth about leadership and team dynamics: every contribution, regardless of its apparent magnitude, plays a vital role in the tapestry of success. As leaders we must learn to look beyond the scoreboard and appreciate the cumulative efforts that drive victories.

Leadership Reflections from the Cricket Field

- **The Foundation Principle**: Every small contribution represents a critical thread in the fabric of success. When leaders fixate solely on grand achievements they risk overlooking the steady, less-visible efforts that make those achievements possible. Like a well-constructed innings, success is built one run at a time.
- **Beyond Traditional Metrics**: While numbers tell part of the story they often fail to capture the intangible contributions that shape outcomes—the morale-boosting words during tough overs, the behind-the-scenes preparation, or the quick thinking that prevents a crisis.
- **The Cumulative Effect**: Exceptional achievements rarely spring from a single moment. They represent the culmination of countless small

actions, decisions, and efforts that pave the way for breakthrough moments. Just as a cricket match isn't won solely in the final over, organisational success is built over time.

- **Psychological Safety and Team Culture**: Recognising and valuing small contributions creates an environment where every team member feels empowered to give their best. This security leads to increased innovation, risk-taking, and overall improved performance.
- **Team Synergy and Collective Success**: Like a well-oiled cricket unit, organisational success demands collective effort. Acknowledging contributions at every level reinforces the interconnected nature of team achievement.

Actionable Leadership Strategies

1. **Recognition Systems:**
   - Implement formal and informal mechanisms to celebrate both standout achievements and essential daily contributions
   - Create platforms for peer recognition and team appreciation
   - Develop regular forums for sharing success stories at all levels
2. **Strategic Storytelling:**
   - Share narratives that highlight the ripple effect of individual efforts

- Document and communicate how small actions contributed to major victories
- Use team meetings to spotlight often-overlooked contributions

3. **Comprehensive Measurement Framework:**
   - Develop tools to capture and evaluate qualitative contributions
   - Create balanced scorecards that include both tangible and intangible metrics
   - Implement regular feedback loops to assess team dynamics and collaboration
4. **Inclusive Culture Building:**
   - Foster an environment where diverse contributions are valued
   - Create opportunities for team members to showcase their unique skills
   - Establish mentorship programmes that emphasize holistic development
5. **Collaboration Enhancement:**
   - Design projects that highlight interdependence and shared success
   - Create cross-functional opportunities for skill sharing
   - Implement team-based rewards alongside individual recognition

Life and Career Coaching Applications

1. **Mindset Development:**
   - Guide clients to recognise and value incremental progress
   - Develop appreciation for the compounding effect of small actions
   - Build resilience through understanding the journey's importance
2. **Recognition Practices:**
   - Implement daily gratitude exercises focusing on small wins
   - Create personal achievement journals
   - Develop peer support networks for mutual encouragement
3. **Skill Enhancement:**
   - Build foundational capabilities that complement core expertise
   - Focus on continuous improvement rather than dramatic changes
   - Create personal development plans that emphasize steady growth
4. **Visualisation Methods:**
   - Guide clients to map small actions to larger objectives
   - Create visual representations of progress and achievement
   - Develop future scenarios that build on current actions

5. **Goal Achievement Strategies:**
   - Break larger objectives into manageable daily tasks
   - Create accountability systems for regular progress
   - Celebrate milestones while maintaining focus on the journey

In the grand game of leadership, success isn't just about celebrating the match-winning six; it's about understanding and valuing every single run that made that six possible. By embracing this principle in life and career coaching, leaders can foster a culture where sustained success becomes not just possible, but inevitable.

Remember, in cricket as in life, it's often the unseen contributions that lay the foundation for visible victories. The key lies in recognising, celebrating, and building upon these crucial building blocks of success.

13

New Boundaries

AT 27, AKHIL found himself on the cusp of change. Life had carved a steady path for him—he had completed probation in a private sector bank and was navigating the beginnings of a career that melded banking operations with his newfound expertise in IT. The cricketing days of his youth, once filled with passion and promise, had faded into cherished memory. Now, his evenings were spent attending seminars, poring over books, or participating in cultural events. Yet beneath this rhythm of progress lingered a quiet yearning for something deeper.

His parents were overjoyed with his steady accomplishments but Baba, ever a man of his word, had a gentle reminder for Akhil one evening.

"Akhil, your time is almost up," he said with a knowing smile.

Akhil froze for a moment before the memory of a promise from two years ago washed over him. "You have two years to find the girl of your dreams," Baba had declared back then. "After that, the choice will be ours." At the time, the words had seemed like a light-hearted challenge, spoken when Akhil was in a steady relationship with Anupama. But as fate would have it, that relationship had ended leaving Akhil to navigate this new phase of his life alone.

Now hearing Baba's words again he couldn't help but smile. "Alright, Baba," he replied with a playful shrug. "It's your challenge now."

With one condition, of course: his partner must not be more than two years younger than him and preferably a *probashi Bangali* like them. Caste, creed, complexion, and looks would not be determining factors. Akhil had learned from his relationship with Anupama that while physical beauty was not insignificant it was the connection of hearts that was much more important.

And so began the search for a partner who could form a meaningful and enduring partnership with Akhil. Matrimonial advertisements were placed in newspapers, and those put up by others were meticulously filtered and sorted by Akhil's parents. Connections began to form, though some progressed only to be abandoned due to incompatibilities in culture, economic status, or expectations.

The search could have stretched endlessly but fate had other plans. Miles away, a gentleman waiting for his train at Sawai Madhopur railway station happened upon a matrimonial advertisement Akhil's parents had placed. Intrigued, he took the ad back to a close family friend who was seeking a suitable groom for his youngest daughter. And so destiny led Akhil's family to Sushmita, a young woman living in the stone city of Kota in Rajasthan.

After several STD calls, letters, and photo exchanges, a meeting was arranged. Sushmita, along with her father and uncle, planned to visit Akhil's home in Banaras on August 15, 1997. Akhil's household prepared to host them, the air buzzing with a mix of anticipation and nervous excitement. While the elders engaged in discussions to gauge family compatibility, Akhil and Sushmita interacted briefly, exchanging only a few words and rarely meeting each other's gaze. Despite his past relationship and several friendships with women, the introverted Akhil was shy around unfamiliar girls. Sushmita too seemed reserved and quiet, adding to the delicate atmosphere of their first meeting.

Sushmita was the youngest of five siblings and embodied everything Akhil's family had hoped for. She was a probashi Bangali from a middle-class family and like them, born and raised in the bustling town of Kota. Her story, much like Akhil's, was one of balancing tradition and modernity, carving out her identity in a world that demanded adaptability for survival.

When Akhil saw her for the first time, it was as though time had paused. Her beauty was undeniable—soft, radiant, and serene. The dimple on her cheek and her large, expressive eyes seemed to hold a world of emotions within them, captivating Akhil instantly. Even the shy Akhil found himself stealing glances at her, careful not to let her notice. There was something about her presence that felt grounding, a calmness that stirred a storm within his heart. She wasn't someone who dazzled a room with her entry; instead, her presence lingered long after she had left. Her absence, Akhil realised, could be felt just as strongly, if not more, than her presence.

She, with her graceful stance, shattered Akhil's belief that love at first sight was a myth. He was smitten.

Following this initial meeting, it was decided that Akhil and his parents, would visit Kota to finalise the marriage. The visit, a few months later, was marked by warmth and mutual respect. Sushmita's family, including her mother, siblings, and close relatives, embraced Akhil's family with open arms. The discussions, though formal, carried an undertone of genuine affection and eagerness to proceed.

Over the next few months, long-distance phone conversations and shared hopes solidified their bond. Akhil's shy nature began to soften in the warmth of Sushmita's quiet but steadfast support. They began to learn about each other, weaving together their dreams and aspirations. Akhil's sense of responsibility towards his partner deepened, much like the camaraderie shared when batting together or bowling in tandem. He reflected on lessons from his past relationships, vowing to explicitly express his admiration and love for Sushmita while also being open about his need for her support.

Her arrival in his life coincided with a blessing—an unexpected opportunity to join a prestigious private bank. The offer came through an old colleague and though it required moving to a new city, Akhil knew it was the right step forward. The City of Joy, Kolkata, would become their new home, marking not just another innings but a new match altogether.

Kolkata was not entirely alien to Akhil. His childhood had been peppered with visits to his maternal grandparents' home during summer vacations and Durga Pujo. The bustling streets, the aroma of street food, and the cultural vibrancy were familiar. Yet moving away from home was a daunting prospect. The comfort of knowing he had some connection to the city provided a small cushion, softening the transition as he prepared to start this new chapter of his life.

The marriage date was set for 25th January the following year. To Akhil, it felt like the announcement of a college tournament—the dates were known and the preparation began, though this time it was all mental and emotional. There were new boundaries to explore and horizons to chase.

Sushmita's presence filled Akhil with a sense of purpose and adventure. Together, they were ready to embark on this journey—partners in life and love, exploring uncharted territories in the quest for a future built on trust, respect, and unwavering support. With her by his side, Akhil knew that this was not the end of his story but the beginning of a beautiful new episode.

Epilogue

THE PREPARATIONS FOR Akhil and Sushmita's marriage began with full fervour. The Banaras home buzzed with excitement, a steady hum of relatives' chatter mingling with the sound of utensils clanging in the kitchen. The air was filled with a sense of purpose but amidst the hustle and bustle, Akhil faced a tough decision—one that required careful negotiation.

Akhil's new employer in Kolkata was eager for him to join immediately. However, his marriage was just two months away, and his current role demanded a three-month notice or monetary compensation equivalent to three months' salary. Caught between professional commitments and personal milestones, Akhil conveyed his dilemma to his soon-to-be boss, hoping for some understanding. After deliberating, the new boss offered a compromise. The company would pay the compensation, but on reflection, he decided against disrupting Akhil's marriage preparations. Instead, he asked Akhil to serve the notice period and join after the wedding. One wicket down, one more to go.

The harder task however was yet to come—informing his current boss Mr. Das of his decision to leave. Akhil had great respect for his employer, a supportive and encouraging leader. For days, he couldn't summon the courage to break the news, feeling a nervousness akin to the days when he had first proposed to Anupama. Eventually, the conversation became inevitable, and Akhil finally mustered the strength to face it. To his surprise, his boss responded with grace and understanding. Though visibly disappointed, he refrained from pressuring Akhil to stay. Instead, he acknowledged that Akhil's new role offered unparalleled opportunities.

"It's sad to see you go, Akhil," his boss said with a wistful smile. "But I'll feel proud watching you grow. Remember, you'll always have a well-wisher here."

These interactions with two seasoned leaders left an indelible mark on Akhil. Their empathy and genuine concern for his well-being exemplified the kind of leader Akhil aspired to become. Their actions were a testament to the respect they commanded, not just for their positions but for their humanity.

With both professional wickets taken, Akhil felt relieved. He threw himself into helping his parents with the wedding arrangements, ranging from organising the guest list to coordinating with caterers and decorators. Despite the whirlwind of activities, Akhil remained dedicated to his current job, ensuring a seamless transition. Grateful for the opportunities his employer had provided, Akhil made sure his departure was smooth and amicable.

The wedding day arrived, bathed in the golden hues of a winter morning. The ceremony unfolded with all the grace and tradition of a Bengali wedding. The '*saat paak*', the '*sindoor daan*', the sacred chants and Ustad Bismillah's Sehnai recitails echoed through the decorated venue as family and friends blessed the couple. Sushmita, draped in a resplendent red Banarasi saree, looked ethereal, her quiet demeanour exuding an inner strength that mesmerised everyone. Akhil, in his traditional *dhoti* and *kurta*, couldn't help but steal glances at his bride, his heart brimming with gratitude and joy.

After the marriage, Sushmita remained in Banaras while her family and friends returned to Kota. She began to take over the household responsibilities from Akhil's mother, who gradually handed her the reins with affectionate guidance. Sushmita also prepared herself for her eventual move to Kolkata by improving her Bangla reading and writing skills and adapting to the nuances of a more cosmopolitan lifestyle.

What no one foresaw was the transformative potential of this quiet and unassuming girl. Sushmita, who moved without fanfare, had an uncanny ability to leave a lasting impression wherever she went. Her small-town simplicity masked an inner resilience that would soon shine through, leaving her footprints on every path she trod.

After completing his notice period, Akhil took a ten-day break. The days were filled with blissful moments spent with Sushmita, preparations for his move to Kolkata, and heartfelt goodbyes to his friends in Banaras. On the designated day, he boarded the train to Kolkata, a city he had visited often during his childhood to see his maternal grandparents during summer holidays and Durga pujo. While the city wasn't entirely unfamiliar, the prospect of living there brought both excitement and apprehension.

The 'City of Joy' was a stark contrast to Banaras. Its bustling streets, iconic yellow taxis, and cultural vibrancy had always charmed him but this time it felt different. Akhil was stepping into uncharted territory, leaving behind the comfort of his hometown and embarking on a new innings of life. Sushmita was to join him in a couple of weeks, once their living arrangements were finalised. Akhil hoped that someday his career might bring him back to Banaras, but for now he was ready to embrace the opportunities Kolkata had to offer.

The initial days in Kolkata were a whirlwind. Akhil threw himself into his new role, navigating the complexities of a larger organisation with determination that left his colleagues impressed. Yet, amidst the professional challenges, his thoughts often wandered to Sushmita. With a couple of STD calls a week that he could afford, he eagerly awaited her arrival, knowing that her presence would bring a sense of completeness to his new life.

When Sushmita finally arrived, the small rented apartment they had arranged instantly felt like home. She brought with her a sense of calm and purpose, transforming the space into a sanctuary. Together they began exploring the city, discovering its hidden gems, and forging their memories. From savouring street food to strolling along the Hooghly River or wandering without any specific destination, every experience deepened their bond.

Sushmita's adaptability amazed Akhil. She quickly found her footing in the bustling city, balancing her traditional values with the demands of a metropolitan lifestyle. Her warmth and humility won over relatives, neighbours, and acquaintances, while her quiet strength became Akhil's anchor in moments of doubt.

Akhil's career flourished in Kolkata, thanks in part to the lessons he'd learnt from cricket, his earlier mentors, and the empathetic leaders he'd encountered. He hoped to someday apply those lessons to his own role, mentoring juniors and building relationships based on trust and respect. Sushmita, too, found her rhythm, contributing to their new life with unwavering support and love.

Over time, Banaras became a cherished memory, a place they visited during holidays to reconnect with their roots. The couple's journey in Kolkata was not without its challenges, but their resilience and partnership carried them through. They learnt to navigate the highs and lows together, holding on to their values, celebrating victories, and finding solace in each other during setbacks.

Looking back, Akhil marvelled at how far they had come. The small-town boy and girl had stepped into the vastness of a metropolis, their hands firmly clasped as they forged a path together. The city that once felt intimidating had become a canvas for their dreams, a place where they built a life filled with love, laughter, and shared aspirations.

As they strolled along, hand in hand one evening, watching the city lights twinkle like a sea of stars, Akhil turned to Sushmita and said, "We've come some way, haven't we?"

Sushmita smiled, her eyes reflecting the same twinkle as the lights below. "And we still have a long way to go," she replied, her voice filled with quiet determination.

With that, they embraced the future—new boundaries to explore, new horizons to chase. Their journey was far from over but together they knew they could face whatever lay ahead. And so the boy from the boundary and the girl who never dragged her feet continued to leave their mark, one step at a time, in the City of Joy.

While cricket had almost faded away from Akhil's life for now, little did they know it would reappear years later, manifesting itself to create new paradigms and new boundaries to explore.

Glossary

Batichokha	a popular traditional Bihari dish that consists of roasted wheat dumplings called "baati" served with a spicy lentil curry known as "chokha." It is also served with spicy mashed potatoes or brinjal, and pickles.
Bhai log	brothers
Bhaiyya	elder brother
Chaat	a family of savoury snacks that originated in India, typically served as an hors d'oeuvre or at roadside tracks from stalls or food carts across South Asia in India, Pakistan, Nepal and Bangladesh. With its origins in Uttar Pradesh, India, chaat has become immensely popular in the rest of South Asia.
dhoti	unstitched garment for men to cover their lower body. It is worn in different ways in different parts of India
Ganne ka ras	sugarcane juice
Golgappa	or panipuri, is a deep-fried breaded hollow spherical shell, filled with a combination of potatoes, raw onions, chickpeas and spices. It is a common snack and street

food in the Indian subcontinent. It is often flavoured with herbs and many other spices.

Guru dakshina a multifaceted concept that embodies a student's gratitude for the knowledge, guidance, and mentorship received from their teacher (guru).

kurta a loose shirt that is a traditional garment for men and women in South Asia. It is often worn with pants, pajamas, or dhoti

Mohalla neighbourhood

prabasi Bangali refers to Bengalis living outside Bengal or born outside Bengal. Based on country, expatriate Bengalis can be divided into expatriate Bangladeshis and expatriate Indian Bengalis.

Riyaz systematic practice of music, dance or any other art form usually under the guidance of a teacher or preceptor.

Saat paak Bengali wedding ritual where the bride and groom encircle the fire seven times, to vow themselves to each other for the next seven lives.

Saptaparni (tree) a small evergreen tree with small greenish-white flowers and a distinctive strong smell that can be observed from December through March in the sub-Himalayan regions of India.

This herb has been used in Ayurvedic, Siddha and Unani medicine for the treatment of various health conditions.

Sindoor daan a Hindu wedding ritual where the groom applies red or orange-red powder to the bride's forehead. It's a mandatory part of a Hindu wedding and signifies the start of a new life for the couple.